11/05

11.99

HOW IT WORKS

HOW IT WORKS
GRAHAM MARKS

BLOOMSBURY

First published in Great Britain in 2004 by Bloomsbury Publishing Plc
38 Soho Square, London, W1D 3HB

The song lyric on p. 205, 'They call us lonely, when we're really just alone' is from
the song *Oblivious* by Aztec Camera, written by Roddy Frame, and is
reproduced by kind permission of Complete Music.

A CIP catalogue record of this book is available from the British Library

ISBN 0 7475 7015 9

Printed in Great Britain by Clays Ltd, St Ives plc

10 9 8 7 6 5 4 3 2

www.bloomsbury.com/HowItWorks

To Nadia, because none of this would have happened without her belief that I could do it. And to Caroline, Justin, Mary, Damian, Philippa, John and Helen, who are the most supportive friends you could wish for.

The image in the photograph I took for the cover was on a junction box round the corner from where I work and just disappeared a couple of days later. I like to think that, in some weirdly cosmic way, it was left there for me to find. Like, I got the angel I deserved, too.

CHAPTER 1

A T HALF PAST EIGHT, SEB'S MOTHER CAME INTO the room again, this time turning on the light and opening the curtains to complete the whole morning scenario. As if he really needed convincing that another bloody day had started.

'Are you going to go to college, or are you just seeing how often the alarm clock goes off before the battery runs out?'

Sunlight and sarcasm, too. Perfect.

'Well?'

'Well what?' Seb's voice sounded as rough as he felt, tongue like a dirty rag, and he coughed as he sat up.

'College.' His mother looked around the room and shook her head.

'What about it?'

'We had a letter this morning about your attendance record.' Seb's mother let the comment hang in the air.

'Right . . .'

'Is that all you've got to say?'

'If I say any more we'll get into it, big time, and I'll be late. Again.'

His mother looked like she really was biting her tongue as she walked over, opened one of the windows, turned and left the room. 'And bring *all* your dirty cups with you when you come downstairs . . .'

* * *

'Fucking great . . .' Since waking up and leaving the house he'd had a mini-argument with his mum – a skirmish setting the battle lines for the real thing when his dad got back from work – a letter from the bank telling him he was £25 overdrawn and would he please get his account back in order as soon as possible (oh, and by the way, we're charging you interest, blah, blah), and now this. He looked back at the screen on his mobile. The text from Shona had just arrived. 'Gudby, and dont call. S' was all it said.

Considering what a shitty day he'd already had, he couldn't say he was totally surprised . . . things were supposed to go in threes. But, even though he and Shona'd had a row yesterday, he wasn't expecting to get dumped. That really capped it.

So, no girlfriend, *less* than no money and everything else going down the pan with his parents. Just the thought of what was waiting for him – getting rinsed by his dad – put even more pressure on him. And imagining his mum looking daggers at him, arms crossed, wishing she could light a fag but she couldn't because she was supposed to have given up, made him worse than pissed off. Hypocrites, both of them. Bloody hypocrites with their Do-as-I-say-not-as-I-do attitudes. What kind of way of life was that? No truth there, just lies and half-truths dressed up to look pretty. They were no better than school, or college, or whatever they wanted to call it. Who could you believe?

Seb looked round at the deserted street, with its trimmed hedges and nice cars and neatly-packed recycling boxes all left out to be taken away and dealt with by someone else. All perfect, on the surface. Everything 'just so', if you played by the rules. Everything lovely if you didn't look too closely. What a bunch of crap.

Life really was a piece of shit sometimes and, standing on the pavement, staring at his phone, he realised this morning was one of those times.

'Fuck it . . . ' he sighed, deleting the text.

Just when you thought things couldn't get any worse, you got a day like today just to prove how wrong you were. The last couple of weeks had been bad, largely because of Martin, and this string of events put the cherry on top.

He'd been introduced to Martin Hill about six months ago, and at first it'd all looked great. Martin was a dealer who had a loose network of contacts moving his stuff about, and people, as he put it, were always dropping off the ladder; as such, he was constantly on the lookout for replacements, and Seb was exactly the kind of person Martin wanted: eager and broke.

To start with, he'd shifted the odd load of Es and been paid in weed. Small stuff, nothing major, twice, maybe three times a month, and he'd ended up with more dope than he could smoke. Which he'd sold on. Then, like almost overnight, he was in deeper and Martin was on the phone to him it seemed like every day to get him to do something. And he was a very hard person to say no to.

Now Seb felt like Martin was taking over his life and, although he didn't have any idea what he actually wanted to do, he knew he didn't want to end up banged up, which is where a lot of people who worked for Martin ended up. There was always the money, but even though he now had a lot more of it, all that meant was that he spent too much.

When it had dawned on him that his life was out of control, being steered by events and other people, he began to get pissed off that he'd absolutely no idea how to change it.

Stuff happened – like Shona leaving him – but it seemed like it was always happening *to* him, not because *he* wanted it to.

Seb stuffed his phone in his back pocket and stood, chewing his lip and wondering what the hell to do next, weighed down by a sense of inevitability. Whatever he did wasn't going to make a difference, so why bother doing anything. And, staring down the street, he knew there were better places than this to do nothing in.

It was getting harder and harder to cheat on the tube, so he'd taken a bus up west. Nowhere particular, just not college or home. Somewhere buzzy, somewhere else. He felt distracted and detached, drifting, kind of like . . . the word dust sprang to mind, and it fit. Dust got blown about, had no control over where it was going but always ended up somewhere, so Seb kept on walking.

He turned a corner and almost bumped into a man who seemed to have taken over the pavement and was using it as his own personal stage. Seb walked round him and stopped to watch him; he was small, not more than five foot six or seven tall, with receding, tightly-curled hair that was going grey, a small moustache and goatee, and clear light blue eyes that darted around the imaginary audience he so plainly was talking to.

The man was speaking very seriously, but whether in some exotic foreign language, or total gibberish, Seb couldn't tell. He also couldn't say how old the man was – a young-looking 45, a badly ageing mid-30s? All he was sure of was that he'd lost the plot, big time.

Spotting a bench outside a nearby supermarket, Seb sat down, leaning forward, his elbows on his knees. He stared at the man, occasionally catching his eye and, when he did, the man just looked straight through him as if he didn't exist. Maybe, right then in his head, in his version of the universe, he didn't. To that man, Seb realised, he probably was invisible.

He'd always found street people fascinating, ever since he could remember. How had they got there? At what point in their lost life did they spin off out of 'normal' orbit and start to nose-dive towards the gutter? And when did they give up trying to climb out and decide that they'd reached their place in what his dad always called 'The Grand Scheme of Things'?

Something must've finally driven this guy nuts, tipped him over the edge. Was everyone born with the crazy seed inside their head, just waiting for the right moment to blossom? He wondered if, with this guy, it was a small thing, the last of *thousands* of small things, that had tipped the balance, or something totally massive that just blew out his circuits. Then he tried to imagine what it would take to mess with his head so much it broke . . . how many days like today would he have to wake up to?

The train of thought was depressing him and he refocused on the madman. The strange thing was, Seb could still see the boy in the man as he carried on waving his arms about just a few metres away. It occurred to him that he'd probably once been some snotty-nosed little kid, growing up in a village thousands of miles and maybe a whole other culture away, running around, chasing his mates. How the hell had he got from that carefree place to here, babbling in whacked-out pidgin English? It didn't make any kind of sense at all.

'Could you move up a little?'

Seb turned and saw a woman standing near him; she had a large, very stylish, black crocodile-pattern leather bag over her shoulder, and was holding a couple of carriers in one hand and take-away coffee and a paper bag in the other.

'No problem.' Seb moved down the bench to give her room, but didn't take his eyes off the performance.

'So much for care in the community.' As the woman put her bags down on the bench between them, she nodded to her right.

Seb didn't realise for a moment that she was talking to him, and then just nodded back. Some people. All they really cared about was that their precious bloody lives weren't affected by anything they didn't like. Later he'd remember that the woman's comment had made him feel sort of negative towards her, kind of explaining why he did what he did. But only kind of.

The madman danced. Seb watched. The woman ate. Her lunch was what looked like a brown bread egg sandwich, and the coffee had a thick brown scum that was all there was left of its failed attempt at being a cappuccino. When the woman finished she very neatly folded the empty sandwich bag into the empty coffee cup and put the plastic top back on; then she very neatly put the cup under the bench.

Care *of* the community, thought Seb.

As she was about to pick up her stuff and go, her mobile went off. She dropped her shoulder bag, fumbled the phone out of her coat pocket and looked at the incoming number before answering.

'Yes, Molly? He's there already? Jesus . . . no, not far away . . . what should you do? Give him one of those bloody herb teas he's so fond of.' Obviously distracted, she reached for her bags without really looking, gathered them together and stood up. 'And put him in Conference 2 . . . I'll be there as fast . . . tell him? I don't know . . . emergency dental appointment, use your bloody imagination, girl!'

Seb glanced over at the bags she was picking up: Karen Millen and Prada. Very stylish dental services.

' . . . Just keep him happy, Molly.' The woman started to walk away. 'Bend over . . . show him some cleavage . . . '

He was just thinking what a real bitch she was when he noticed something on the bench beside him. It was a black crocodile-pattern wallet that matched the shoulder bag. It must've fallen out when she put her bag down, and he knew he should call out after her. But he didn't. In fact, without even glancing round to see if anyone was watching, he picked up the wallet, put it in his jacket pocket and, with one last look at the loony tune, walked away in the opposite direction.

He'd never stolen anything before, anything of real value that belonged to an actual person. In broad daylight. It felt weird, he was excited and paranoid at the same time . . . massively in control and completely disconnected from reality in one breath. He was sitting on another bench now, this one on the large, triangular traffic island, a kind of no-man's land where a whole bunch of roads met. There was a theatre over to his left and a row of faceless office buildings in front of him, and a constant stream of cars wherever you looked, like metal sharks, hunting pedestrians.

Seb looked around for any signs of trouble. He was alone, apart from the sleeping figure on another bench; there were five empty lager cans on the ground by his head and a puddle where he must've pissed himself. No trouble there, then.

Getting the wallet out, Seb cradled it on his lap. Guilt made him feel very exposed, like there were eyes everywhere, watching every move he made. He looked inside. There were a dozen cards – credit, cheque guarantee, store, loyalty. You name it, Sara Hawkins had one. She also had a shedload of cash. £235. Two-hundred-and-thirty-five-pounds. Count 'em.

He took a deep breath. He could do one of three things . . . hand the wallet in, claiming he'd found it, complete with the cards and the money; he could hand it back with the cards and just keep the money. Or he could keep everything. Seb checked through the wallet again and behind the HSBC bank card he found a small piece of paper with four numbers written on it.

'Bloody hell . . . ' he whispered. 'Stupid cow keeps her PIN code with her card . . . '

Standing outside the bank, Seb didn't know how he felt. Relieved that he'd got away with getting the money out of the cash machine – another £75, all the account would let him have – or scared at what he was doing. It was like he was living someone else's life, someone like Dean South, who'd been chucked out of school in Year 11 for general hoodlum behaviour and thieving from school lockers in particular.

The thing to do, he'd figured out over the last 45 minutes, was *not* to think about how he felt, or what he was doing, but just go with the flow. Deal with the consequences later. No point in worrying, no point at all. He had money in his pocket, he had credit cards, he had the rest of the day to let rip . . . but before he did that he decided to do something sensible. He went to a branch of his own bank and paid £200 into his account to clear the overdraft and then some, giving him a nice bit of breathing space.

Somewhere in Seb's head there was still a tiny, sane voice whispering instructions. He listened, and then he hit the pubs.

'Hello?'

Silence.

'Is anyone there? . . . I can't help you unless you say something . . . '

The voice sounded nothing like the photo, and that had stopped Seb in his tracks. He'd taken ages to take his pick – too much choice, like at the sweet counter in the newsagents – and now, because the voice didn't sound the way he expected, he didn't know what to do.

'I'll have to put the phone down, sir, other customers.'

'No! Um, you don't sound, you know . . . ' Young, is what he meant, but he didn't want to say it.

'I just take the calls.'

'What do I do . . . make an appointment?'

'Where are you?'

'Just off Drury Lane.'

'You're five minutes away, sir.' The woman sounded bored. 'Come right round.'

Seb put the phone down after he'd taken directions and stared at the tart card he had in his hand.

Crazy Janey – 19 yrs old, all services, hotel visits – genuine photo

He stuffed it in the back pocket of his jeans, wondering why he'd chosen that particular girl . . . maybe, he thought, because she looked the most ordinary, despite calling her-self 'crazy'. With one last look at *Beautiful Portuguese Dish*, *Tina – Try Me – New Girl in Town!*, *Sophie – Beautiful, Dedicated and Dark!* and the truly odd *Best Nipples in Town,* he left the phone box.

CHAPTER 2

BEHIND HIM, SEB HEARD GIRLS LAUGHING AT something. The quiet little voice inside his head whispered that they were laughing at him, and he nearly turned round to go to the tube station and home territory. Nearly, but not quite. He was on a roll, the day was no way over yet; it wasn't even midnight and he felt like he had a mission to complete – he was nowhere near close enough to the edge.

Minutes later, he was standing outside a building with the tarnished brass numbers 58–60 on the scuffed blue door and a hand-written label saying 'Flat 7' by the top left-hand bell. That's what she'd said, so this must be the place. Seb swayed slightly as he stood in front of the door, trying hard to focus on the cracks in the paint. He took a deep breath and shook his head to clear it. The fact that he really needed to take a leak was the deciding factor that made him finally press the bell.

'Hello?'

'It's me . . . I, um, phoned earlier?'

'Come up, sir.'

The tinny speaker went dead and the door buzzed. Seb pushed it and went in, thinking he quite liked being called 'sir'.

*   *   *

He hadn't known what to expect, but he certainly hadn't thought it would be ordinary. He was sitting on the edge of a saggy old armchair in a badly-lit room with a blue-green swirly carpet and brown, geometric-pattern wallpaper, looking at a startlingly blonde, very pale woman who was old enough to be his mum. Although his mum, or any of the women of that age he knew, would never, in a million years, be like this. She looked, in her high-necked, frilly red blouse, tight black leather skirt and teased hair, like the kind of bit-part player you'd see in the background on *EastEnders*, and she was standing by an old, Formica-topped dresser, lighting a cigarette.

'She won't be long,' the woman nodded towards a door on the other side of the room. 'I'd offer you a drink, but you look like you've had a few already, dear . . . don't want to let yourself down, do you . . . '

'No . . . ' said Seb, who'd asked to use the toilet as soon as he'd made it up to the fourth floor, and was now feeling far too sober and like he really could use another drink. The longer he waited, the less he felt like going the distance.

'How old are you anyway?'

'19.' Well, he thought, almost.

'Right . . . ' the woman raised an eyebrow. 'So what are you after, sir? Full service, something special?'

Seb looked at her, blankly.

'Sir can make a deposit, if you'll pardon the pun,' the woman smiled, took a long drag and blew smoke out of her nose, 'and we'll settle up after.'

'How much?' asked Seb, getting up and taking his wallet out of his back pocket.

'£50, that's the basic, any extras, we'll settle up afterwards.'

As Seb took five crisp tens out of the wad he still had left, the door to what he assumed was the bedroom opened and a man wearing a creased suit and a wide grin appeared, straightening his tie. He didn't even glance at Seb on his way out.

'Silent, but golden,' the woman nodded, putting Seb's money in a drawer. 'Your turn, sunshine . . .'

Seb looked at the door, wondering why this had all seemed like such a good idea not so very long ago. Is that what you did when the world and your girlfriend dumped on you? Paid for a shag? What was he like? He looked at the woman, her face waxen in the flare of the lighter sparking up another fag. She didn't seem the kind of person you could ask that sort of question – like she'd care – or one who'd give you your money back if you'd had a change of heart. And something right deep down just wouldn't let him wimp out and leave.

'Half an hour, sir,' the woman said as he finally stepped towards the door, 'no more . . .'

Seb stood on the pavement, both hands in his jacket pockets against the cold. Behind him he heard the scuffed blue door click shut. The thin, wiry man with the iron grip, the one standing right next to him holding his arm tight, coughed and spat.

'You better bloody be telling the truth.'

'Look, you got all my money, all the cards . . .' the man's fingers were digging into his upper arm, ' . . . and I told you, the account's empty!'

'I'm gonna believe a thieving little bugger like you?' The man pulled Seb with him as he set off down the street.

Seb slouched along next to the man. He had narrow,

slitted eyes that never seemed to stop searching, and lank, greasy, dark hair, cut short at the front, long at the back, and he talked with an accent that Seb thought could be Russian. Full circle, he thought. Everything had gone right round to where it was in the morning. Back to square one. Crap.

He'd been properly set up. The woman must've spotted the cards in his wallet when he paid her . . . must've phoned someone. End result: this vicious little bastard had been waiting for him when he'd come out of the room, and that was it. Wallet emptied, cards taken and then he'd been slapped around a bit until he'd told them how come he'd got a load of stuff that wasn't his. They'd believed that part of the story, him and the blonde woman, but they weren't convinced when he told them there was nothing left to take out of Sara Hawkins's account.

And all the time, Janey — if that was her name — had stayed well out of it all. Which, right now, is what he wished he'd done. There were any number of times he could've bailed out of the madness today but, with his beer head and fuck-you attitude, he'd ignored every opportunity.

It was now well after midnight and, although there were still people on the streets, he didn't think it would do him much good calling for help. The man — Zack, the blonde woman had called him — kept a firm hold on him and constantly moved his head from side to side, scanning like he had radar.

'There's a load of machines round the corner,' he muttered, pulling Seb along faster. 'Something there for everyone.'

'But I told you . . . '

'Shut it, or you'll wish you had . . . '

* * *

Everything hurt. Seb felt colder than he'd ever felt before, lying curled up in a ball on the filthy stone slabs of a West End pavement; he knew he had to move, and he also had a fair idea that no one was going to lift a finger to help him do it. He'd walked past enough down-and-outs himself to know that for an actual fact.

Zack had been pissed off to hell when he found out there really was no more money. Really took it personally, pushing Seb into an alley and working him over like he was a punchbag in a gym. He'd tried to fight back – had landed a couple of good hits and a nasty little shin kick that must've hurt – but he wasn't a natural dirty fighter. He couldn't compete. He went down, bleeding and scared, half-convinced this psycho-maniac was going to finish him off after he'd taken a booting in the kidneys. Then, for whatever reason, Zack stopped, and left him where he fell. Really in the shit now.

It took Seb a long time to get upright, longer still to get out of the alley. Shivering, he stood, leaning against a wall. Through the one eye that was still open he tried to work out where he was and which way would lead him home – although how he'd get there was another matter. He had nothing, not even enough change for a phone call. And even if he had, he wasn't sure he could talk, and couldn't think who he'd call. Seb looked at his watch, which he thought said it was about 1.45 in the morning. His parents would go ballistic, and that was the last thing he needed right now. Shona wasn't talking to him, and he wasn't sure any of his mates would drop everything to come and get him.

That particular thought made him feel even worse, and he had no idea whether the hot tears running down his cheeks were from the pain, or the fact that he couldn't think of a single person who'd help. Then, through the fog of hurt, he remembered his mobile. He fumbled it out of the inside pocket of his jacket and was amazed to see that it had come through the ordeal seemingly unscathed. He'd switched it off before going up to the flat, for some reason worried he might get called at the wrong moment, the weirdness of his logic only now occurring to him.

Seb turned it back on, punched in his security code and watched the display as it searched for a connection. Still no one to call, he thought, as the phone locked on, picking up that he had a missed call and a text. Though not completely abandoned, either. He thought about seeing who'd been trying to get in touch, but suddenly realised he was shivering so badly he really should find some kind of shelter.

Clutching a large polystyrene cup of vegetable soup in both hands, Seb felt the warmth penetrate his achingly cold body, bit by bit. It tasted wonderful. So good he could feel the tears welling up in his eyes again.

He glanced around, taking in the strange, post-apocalyptic scene he'd stumbled across near Embankment tube station . . . the soup van, parked under a street lamp in the middle of the night, with the couple of blokes doling out cups to a ragged-arsed group of losers and misfits. He felt right at home. No one, except the soup boys, attempted to make eye contact and everyone, apart from the soup boys, looked like life had dealt them an awesomely bad hand of cards.

Seb finished the soup, then remembered the slab of bread he'd been given and had put in his pocket so he could warm both hands on the cup. Maybe he could get a refill to dunk the bread in. Maybe the blokes running the van might be going north when they'd finished; they might give him a lift nearer home, if he told them, sort of, what had happened to him. But maybe they'd heard every story there was and would just nod and smile. Whatever. He had to try.

'S'cuse me.' Seb held out his cup, feeling like Oliver Twist.

'Second helpings in twenty minutes, mate,' said one of the blokes, a guy with a shaved head and two large silver earrings in each ear.

'Give the latecomers a chance, you know?' said the other bloke.

'OK, but . . . '

'Twenty minutes, mate, you'll have to wait, like everyone else.'

'I was only . . . ' Before he could finish explaining, Seb was roughly shouldered out of the way by a large man with long, matted hair and a straggly beard, who was draped in a filthy blue sleeping bag.

'Fuck off and die, new boy,' he grunted, reaching out a bandaged hand and taking some soup and a slice of bread. 'We got rules . . . '

Seb limped back into the shadows, aware that he was now the object of unwanted interest. He had to stay nearby because he really needed a second helping of soup, and a second chance to ask for a favour, but meanwhile he felt it would be a good idea if he got himself out of the spotlight.

He leant against some railings, exhausted. His head, like the rest of him, was a mess, and he couldn't seem to keep a thought in focus long enough for it to connect with anything and have meaning. Everything was random, a chaotic jumble of incidents and emotions that kept running through his mind like some insane film that had no storyline, no script, no point. Like a dream, really, a very, very bad dream. Except he knew it was all real, and none of it was anything to be proud of, and he probably deserved to be where he was, feeling as shitty as he was, right now.

Then, in the middle of trying to make sense of a totally surreal day, his phone started to ring. Because this didn't immediately make sense, Seb looked at his watch first – it was 2.30am – and only then dug the phone out of his pocket and saw that it was his home number calling. He felt so cold, so tired, so sick of what was happening to him that he didn't care how much he got yelled at as long as someone came and got him, and he pressed the answer key.

'So the fuckin' new boy's got a mobile, has he?'

Seb looked up and saw the man wrapped in the sleeping bag coming towards him. He was transfixed by the arc the white polystyrene cup made as the man threw it away, the soup flying out and cutting a dull orange slash across the night sky.

'What you doin'?' the man was roaring as he ran at Seb, fists flying. 'Cheapskate toffee-nose bastid, come here, take our food, pretend to be fuckin' homeless!'

The last thing Seb remembered thinking, as the man began laying into him, was that he really didn't want to die. Not here. Not now . . .

CHAPTER 3

COMING TO, SEB WAS AWARE OF HIS BODY switching back on, bit by bit, like a house gradually being illuminated, one room at a time. Everything was there – he could feel pain, lots of pain, he could smell, hear, taste and he was aware of light – but nothing seemed to work properly . . . it was as if he'd been parcelled up in barbed wire and bubble-wrap. Not a great feeling, but at least he was alive.

He was conscious that there were people near him, but he found his eyes wouldn't open, so he couldn't see who they were and he couldn't quite make out what they were saying which, combined with the fact that he also couldn't make his mouth work, was so completely frustrating he stopped trying. Instead, he concentrated on his other big problems . . . where was he, and how had he got there?

Hospital was the likely answer to question one, with 'by ambulance' the obvious follow-on if that were true. But who had made it happen? The guys running the soup van? Then he remembered the last thing he'd been doing before the crazed Wookie with the blue sleeping bag had attacked him. Answering a call from home. And he'd just picked up when the fun started, so his mum, or dad, had probably heard all of whatever had happened. Must've been those blokes, somehow.

Thinking it might be them in the room with him, Seb attempted to move, talk and open his eyes, all at the same time. All he managed to achieve was jacking his pain quotient up so far that he passed out again.

'I think he's waking up, shall I go and tell them?'

'Let's wait and see what kind of state he's in, shall we . . . we don't know yet if there'll be any long-term effects . . . he's taken a hell of a pounding.'

'Pulse is strong . . . blood pressure fine, all vital signs stable now . . . '

'Turn the lights down, nurse . . . he's going to find the light a bit harsh.'

'Reflexes seem to be working fine.'

'Good . . . have you lowered the morphine?'

'Yes . . . it's been coming down steadily since this morning.'

It was some time before Seb realised the voices he could hear were possibly talking about him, and that he hadn't fallen asleep while watching *Casualty*. If it *was* him they were talking about, he must be in a pretty bad way.

This time, he thought, he'd do things slowly. Which was a good move, as opening his eyes was a big effort. In the dimly-lit room he could see figures moving about . . . two, no, three of them . . . dressed in white . . . he could see tubes and wires snaking away from his body and he was aware of machines ticking and sighing in the background. The whole thing was like being in an alien abduction episode of *X-Files*, with him as Fox Mulder.

'Where am I?' Not the most original question, but simple. Seb moved his hand in a kind of questioning wave. There, he'd opened his eyes, spoken and moved. And he was still awake.

'University College Hospital, Sebastian.'

Somebody called him Sebastian. Couldn't see who. Hadn't been called that for years.

'How do you feel?' Different voice, a woman's, nearer. He turned towards it.

'Been better.'

'I hope so,' said the woman, whose face was level with his. 'We have to do some tests . . . make sure everything's OK before we get your parents in. This won't take a minute . . . '

Seb's mum and dad hadn't stayed long. Long enough, though, for his mum to lose it and have to be taken out by a nurse. Which left him with his dad. Not his first choice of bedside companions. Especially as he was now able to remember most of what had happened to him and was in no mood to try and explain himself.

His dad, not much good at doing warm, emotional stuff at the best of times, was completely stymied now that Seb was in no condition to have his back slapped in a sporty kind of way. So he asked the first question, to break the silence and get the ball rolling.

'How long've I been here?'

'God . . . let me think . . . I've kind of lost track . . . four days, it's been four days . . . '

Four days!

' . . . it was touch and go for the first 24 hours, they said, and you did look terrible . . . your mother's been beside herself, been off work ever since, spent most of the time here . . . I've come as often as I could, but there's been all the print for a conference to organise and . . . '

'It's OK, Dad, really.' Seb actually felt he should be the one comforting his father, and tried to reach out.

'Lucky your friend turned up, really, otherwise . . . ' His dad's voice caught as he put his hand out and patted Seb's, ' . . . otherwise they said you might not have made it.'

Friend?

After his dad went, Seb was left on his own with just the ticking, sighing machines to keep him company. And the puzzling fact that someone, he had absolutely no idea who, had apparently saved his life. It made him feel weird, suddenly cold in the over-warm room.

In the low light, surrounded by the mechanics and science of medicine, the scent of doctoring pricking his nostrils, the enormity of nearly dying flooded through him. He could feel his heart thumping in his chest, blood pounding in his ears and hear his breath coming in short, panicky, sharp bursts. Then, somewhere in the background, he heard a high-pitched electronic beeping . . .

The woman doctor, the one he'd woken up to find looking at him, was sitting on the edge of his bed, glancing at her watch. She looked tired, Seb thought, as she reached behind her and picked up the clipboard with his notes on it. The two nurses and the other doctor who'd all rushed into his room when the alarm had gone off had left now that he'd stabilised.

'I've no idea what brought that on.' She pushed a trailing shank of hair back behind her ear as she looked at his notes.

'What was it?'

'No idea . . . something pushed your heart rate sky high for a moment or two.' She looked up. 'But you seem to have settled down now . . . I don't know if you realise quite how lucky you are to be with us, and in what appears to be fairly decent working order . . . no permanent damage, as far as we can tell.'

'Yeah . . . my dad said . . . he also told me a friend helped me . . . d'you know, um, can you tell me who it was?'

The doctor – Seb could see from her name badge that she was called Dr McCain – looked at him slightly oddly. 'Don't you remember who you were with?' She scanned the clipboard. 'Are you suffering from much memory loss?'

Not nearly enough, thought Seb, who, by now, had remembered every tiny detail of a day he'd much rather forget. 'No . . . I can remember everything . . . I just wasn't with anyone I know . . . not all day.'

'Well, whoever it was, he was the one who came with you here to the hospital.' Dr McCain flicked through some pages before putting the clipboard back down. 'His name's not here with the medical notes . . . I'll find it when I come back on duty tomorrow, if that's all right.'

'Sure . . . ' Seb wasn't able to hide his disappointment very well. 'Did you meet him?'

'No, but I think Nurse Owen did.' The doctor got up and collected her stethoscope from the trolley next to his bed. 'I'll ask her to look out his name and come and talk to you, OK?'

'Thanks.'

'See you tomorrow . . . '

Nurse Owen was a mine of information, most of it to do with the catalogue of injuries Seb'd sustained. Multiple lacerations, bruised everything, a cracked rib, delicate kidneys and a couple of loose teeth, ' . . . plus they *thought* you'd got a possible blood clot that could have led to permanent brain damage,' she said, as she finished counting off the staggering list of woes that had befallen him.

'You shoulda seen the other guy . . . ' Seb gave her a slightly lopsided grin.

'*He* was taken to another hospital, not sure which,' said Nurse Owen, brightly. 'Your friend broke his jaw, apparently, and it still took four people to hold him down!'

Seb stared at the nurse, frowning. 'This friend . . . '

'The one you don't remember?'

'I don't remember him cos he wasn't there right up till I blacked out . . . I told you!'

'I believe you, I believe you . . . '

'So who was he? Dr McCain says you saw him.'

'Only for a moment . . . I was too busy with you.' Nurse Owen looked down at a piece of paper on her lap. 'I looked up the notes . . . they say his name's Jay Brill . . . '

'Wonder what the J stands for?'

'No, it's J,A,Y – Jay, the name.' She showed him the piece of paper with it written down. 'Funny name, really, for an English bloke . . . more of an American name, don't you think?'

'He was English?'

'Sounded it.'

'What did he look like?'

'Wasn't paying much attention . . . you were in such a mess, blood everywhere and such a faint pulse . . . '

'Was he tall, short, fat?'

'He was just sort of ordinary looking.' She looked away at the wall, as if trying to project a picture of him on to it so she could describe him better. 'Normal sort of height, brownish hair . . . bit long. . . I do remember he had a nice smile . . . '

'How old was he?'

'Oh, I dunno,' Nurse Owen smiled, 'I'm dreadful with people's ages . . . about 30-something?'

Seb nodded, watching her as she looked down at the watch pinned to her uniform and then got up, smoothing her skirt.

'Back to work?' he asked.

'My last night shift for two whole weeks,' Nurse Owen smiled as she fussed around the bed, tidying it up and checking all the bits that were still attached to Seb. 'No offence, but I can hardly wait to get away!'

'See you, then . . . '

'I'll look in before I go.'

Watching the door close behind her, Seb felt exhausted and tense at the same time, and as he made himself relax it was almost as if the pillows were pulling him down. He let them. Right now he was in a complete limbo, somewhere between the total extinction of dreamless sleep and the harsh reality he knew was grinding on outside the safety of the hospital walls. Soon, how soon he had no idea, he was going to have to leave and face the rest of his life. A life, he'd been told, that he'd have lost but for his 'friend'.

'Jay Brill . . . ' he whispered, wondering who the hell he could be. Just some passing good Samaritan who, at some ungodly hour of the morning, had waded in and plucked him out of the gutter? Unless he was suffering from memory loss – and, with incidents from that fucked-up day flashing, unwanted, through his head, he was pretty damn sure he wasn't – he had no idea who the man was.

Nurse Owen's description was worse than useless: a

normal-looking, 30-something bloke who was probably English, needed a haircut and had a nice smile. Not a lot to go on. But he did have a name, which, she was right, was a bit of an odd one. And, now he came to think about it, it did sound American, like that chat show host on cable . . . Jay Leno, was it?

'Jay Brill . . . ' He tried saying it again, as if that might dislodge a memory, hidden away in some recess, and help to conjure a picture in his head. It didn't, although there was some comfort in knowing what this stranger was called . . . he felt less spooked now he had a name.

Seb didn't want to think of what was going to be waiting for him once he got home and the questions started. He wasn't going to be let off lightly, and he knew he was mostly to blame . . . if he was going to be brutally honest, that particular set of circumstances was almost entirely his own creation, although he didn't think that he'd ever admit that, to anyone.

All he did know, as he slipped off to sleep, was that if there was one thing he absolutely had to do, it was to find the mysterious Mr Brill and thank him. He owed him, big time . . . but how the hell, he thought, do you ever repay a life?

CHAPTER 4

DURING THE TIME HE'D SPENT IN HOSPITAL, SEB had had plenty of opportunity to think and to plan and decide what to do when he got out. Plenty of opportunity, but no inclination. He'd been kind of left alone by his parents . . . they'd visited, of course, but nothing had been said, and he felt they wanted to talk about what had happened as little as he did.

Thing was, when he did get out, he was still stuck at home. Although the cuts and bruises had all but disappeared, leaving a few trace scars, his breaks were mending really well and he thought he was feeling fine, everyone else seemed to be very worried about him.

So, as far as Seb could tell, he wouldn't be going back to college till just before the end of the spring term, just in time to fail his A levels and really screw things up. Which was why he'd begun, with no prompting, to revise. He couldn't handle the thought that he might sink any further than rock bottom.

He'd had enough time on his own now, put enough distance between himself and what his parents were now referring to as 'the incident', to have figured out a few things. Like the fact that he had no idea where he was going, or what he was going to do when he eventually got there.

*   *   *

Spending time alone had never been a problem for him, in fact he'd always wished his parents, particularly, had given him more space. Before, he'd filled his time with pretty much nothing. Computer games, music, TV. Nothing he paid much attention to, nothing that went anywhere or made any difference.

Now was just about the same, except that, now, he didn't know why, he felt he owed it to himself to pass English and art, even if he had no bloody idea what good it was going to do him. In fact, he'd only opted for those subjects because they weren't too difficult and he disliked them the least. Which wasn't, he knew, much of a way to make a career choice.

On his own at home, he still did all the same mindless things as before, but as he did them he found himself, without intending to, imagining he was fully recovered. He figured it might have something to do with having a purpose: finding Mr Brill. Because he couldn't do that stuck at home.

Having a purpose, he realised, was the major difference. It felt odd, having something important to do, even if it only really mattered to him. In the end, all he wanted to do was to say thank you.

'Thank you, Mr Jay Brill, for probably saving my life and not letting me die in some gutter.'

It wasn't what you'd call a quest, and he certainly didn't feel he deserved saving, after how he'd spent the day in question.

That thought kept on coming back, like a dog to its empty bowl, sniffing round his brain, searching for an answer, or at least a reason, as to why *him*. Why was he any better than any of the other people out there who needed pulling out of the slow plunge to oblivion that their lives had become? There had been a dozen or more *real* down-and-outs right there by the soup van to choose from. People who were probably far more deserving. So why him?

Chance. Luck. Fate. Destiny. Coincidence. Take your pick, he thought, because they all had the same meaning as throwing dice. Which was precisely none. Meeting Jay Brill would mean he could ask him why he'd stepped in. It wouldn't change anything, he still wouldn't know where he was going, but at least he would know what the answer was, even if the reply was 'just because'. At least he would have done something.

'Hello?'

'Seb, that you?'

'Yeah . . . '

'Just calling to see how you were, mate.'

Silence.

'So, how are you?'

'Yeah, fine, you know . . . '

'Feeling better?'

'Not bad.'

'Anything you need?'

'What d'you want, Martin?'

'That's nice, isn't it . . . call up for a chat, see how you are.'

'Leave me alone, Martin.'

Hang up.

There was one thing Seb had learnt, or at least thought might be true about human beings: by and large, to use a well-worn phrase of his dad's, they preferred things the way they were. Did not like change. Would do a lot to make sure stuff remained the same. It was, he thought, a kind of safety catch – keep it firmly locked on and nothing bad would happen. No loud bangs. The status quo would remain the same.

Everyone wanted things to be the same. Martin wanted him back shifting stuff for him, and his parents wanted to ignore reality, like, if you didn't talk about something in any way, shape or form (another of his dad's pet mutterings) it would get bored and go away. Just like 'the incident'.

Seb realised that he was exactly the same, too. He did not want to talk to his parents about what had happened, and he also hoped that, given enough time, 'the incident' would be forgotten, packed away in the family vault of 'things best left unsaid'. Except that part of him was desperate to talk to someone about it.

It was all still too real, like the worst kind of nightmare. But, the further he moved in time away from it, the harder it became to put what had happened into words, even in his head. He didn't believe the images would ever go away, but it might help if he talked about them. Thing was, he couldn't think of anyone he could count on to trust with the story.

'Seb?'

'Leave me alone, Martin.'

'It's not polite to put the phone down on someone . . . I thought better of you, I really did.'

'I can't do anything for you Martin, I'm still not better.'

'I understand that, just give me a bell when you are, OK?'

'Yeah, OK . . . '

He wished Martin would just fade away, but he knew that wasn't going to happen. Manic Martin, that's what some people called him, because when he got something in his head he kept on and on at it, simply wouldn't let go. And it seemed to Seb that getting him back on the team had fallen fair and square into that category.

Apart from Martin, Seb's only contact with the outside world had been when a couple of his mates had come round to see him. Damon and Jack. Good blokes, really, but all they'd wanted to do was look at his scars and talk about how much they'd drunk the previous weekend and how sick Tanya and Celine had been at some bloke's party. Even if he'd wanted to, Seb couldn't see himself telling them what had happened, downloading in a caring, sharing way; all they'd want was details, the scuzzier the better, about what he'd been up to. Wasn't going to happen.

And Shona. Not a bloody peep out of her. Not even a stupid text. She couldn't even be bothered to do that, the cow. He'd thought that maybe she was waiting for him to get in touch with her, but then Jack had said she'd got herself a new boyfriend. He worked in a bank. Had his own car. Apparently. So it was goodbye to Shona. Hoo-bloody-ray.

His mate Tim had called, once. He'd had a card from Soppy Anna, who he knew had fancied him since Year 7, but there was no way . . . no way ever in the world. His older brother, Tony, had e-mailed him from sunny Florida, where he worked for a big marketing company. He'd sent all his best, and hoped Seb's exams went OK. Which was nice. And that was it since he'd come home from hospital, which, he realised, didn't say much for his social skills.

The most he'd talked was when he was in hospital, mainly to Nurse Owen, whom he'd continually pestered with questions about Jay Brill, and also Dr McCain. She'd kept a running check on him right up till he'd left, there so often it almost seemed like he were her special patient. It was during one of her visits that she'd let slip he'd been given an AIDS test.

An AIDS test?

He was stunned at first, then figured it must have been because of the mad bloke who'd trashed him, because of all the blood, and that he might have been HIV positive. But that wasn't the case. His friend, said Dr McCain, had pointed out the card stuffed down in the back pocket of his jeans, the Crazy Janey one he'd taken from the phone booth, and she'd thought they'd better be on the safe side. After a moment's nervous silence on his part he'd asked what the results were.

'You're fine,' Dr McCain looked straight at him. 'This time.'

He'd wanted to say that he didn't usually do this kind of stuff. That he wasn't the kind of bloke who went out looking for trouble, got drunk and slept with prostitutes. He wanted, for some reason he couldn't work out, for Dr McCain to like him and be taking extra care of him because she liked him. But you could never tell with doctors. Getting people well again was what they did. It was their job. They did it whether you were the world's biggest shit, or Mother Teresa.

That kind of attitude took commitment, and Seb couldn't think of anything, or anyone, he'd ever been committed to. He realised he didn't believe in anything strongly enough to give him direction, a target, something to aim for. He thought about the people in his life as well, probably for the first time looking at them . . . what was the word? Objectively. As if from a distance, as if he had no connection with them.

He didn't find it difficult to do, which at first surprised

him. And then he worked out that it was because he wasn't really close to anyone, that the distance was already there. He could sort of see why with his parents, who had always seemed to be at arm's length, and his friends, who were the blokes he laughed at the same jokes with, which was kind of the full extent of his link with them. But with someone like Shona, who he had been sleeping with? How could you be so close, physically, but not in your head?

Did this make him a bad person? Hard question. To which in the end he answered no, it just made him like lots of other people. Hard to like. Hard to love, to be more accurate. And easier to dump.

'Seb? Look, I need to know like *when* you're gonna be up for some work.'

'Martin, I . . . '

'Gotta have the smart boy back, right?'

'I can't . . . '

'Got plans for you, Seb . . . I can spot talent.'

'I don't want to . . . '

'I'm surrounded by such bozos it's doing my head in, Seb! No word of a lie, mate . . . so, will it be next week some time?'

'You're stressing me out, Martin . . . I'll call you, OK?'

'Yeah, yeah, call me . . . can't you tell me now?'

'No, Martin . . . I can't.'

Seb sat back, wishing Martin could find it as easy to forget him as the other people in his life. The hardest part about being on his own so much was that he couldn't forget, he couldn't turn his mind off, because once he started thinking about something, like what the hell he was going to do about Martin, it just went on and on and on. Maybe that was why they called it a train of thought? Carriage after carriage of often disconnected things going on down the line, destination unknown. It made him feel slightly schizo, having these deep conversations with himself in his head, sometimes even wondering if he got so involved he wasn't actually talking out loud.

Blitzing the revision helped stop the thinking, helped stun the brain into submission and halt the flow of unwanted conclusions. Like, he was a shit, which was why no one really cared. Except someone did care. Someone he didn't know, but who obviously knew about him . . . like, exactly how *did* Mr Brill know about the card in his jeans pocket? Had he been following Seb all that day? Had he seen *everything* he'd got up to?

Had he been following him for longer, even?

That was the kind of thought Seb found made him really edgy, the kind of thought that hung around like a bad smell and just wouldn't go away. Maybe Mr Jay Brill was a complete weirdo who he'd be better off not meeting. Ever. You kept hearing about stuff like that every day, just about. Freaks who got obsessive and ended up topping the person they had a thing for.

But if that was the case, why save him in the first place?

Backwards and forwards, round and round, circles within circles. If he didn't get out of the house soon, he was going to go certifiably nuts. Like Martin.

'Seb!'

'What?'

'You've left your mobile down here and it's ringing . . . want me to answer it for you?'

'No, Mum . . . leave it – does it say who's calling?'
'Martin?'
'Oh . . . '
'Seb?'
'What?'
'Are you coming for this phone or what?'
'No . . . let it take a message . . . '
'Who's Martin, do I know him?'
'No.'

CHAPTER 5

EVERY DAY, AT SOME POINT, SEB WOULD STOP WHAT he was doing and get out his wallet. He'd sit for a while, just holding it, aware that, apart from his mobile, it was the only thing he still owned from that night. Sort of a souvenir, in a weird, twisted kind of way. He'd got a whole bunch of new clothes and stuff, as everything he'd been wearing his mum had taken home while he was still in hospital and he'd never seen any of it again.

The day he'd left to go home, Nurse Owen had handed over his wallet and phone, warning that he might find 'a bit of blood still in the keypad'. He'd been momentarily transfixed when he'd thought that the woman's – Sara Hawkins – credit cards were still in his wallet. Anyone even remotely curious should have found them, and he was sure someone at the hospital must've searched through all his belongings when he'd been brought in.

Seb had opened his wallet, wondering why he hadn't been asked about how come he was in possession of credit cards that weren't his. Simple. It turned out they weren't there. Confused, it had been a couple of minutes before he remembered that Zack had taken them. Maybe he was suffering from some memory loss if he'd forgotten that.

*   *   *

Each time Seb looked at the folded square of soft, brown leather, it brought everything back into sharp focus, and he began to wonder about Jay Brill, about what he'd done and why on earth he'd done it. Fact was, the man could have ended up in hospital himself by getting involved, could've been badly hurt. Weird.

And the other thing he found odd was that, so far, nothing had touched him. Of all the bad things that could have come down on him, the worst was a mild slap on the wrist for his appalling school attendance record and generally crappy attitude. Why he'd ended up at a street soup van at two in the morning, no one had thought to ask. Everything, the thieving, the whoring and the boozing, seemed to have been swept away by the violence of the attack – no one ever realising that it was the second beating he'd taken that night.

The thing of it was, though the visible effects of the assault and battery were healing well, almost gone in many cases, his memory was still scarred. He could feel himself, like a kid, picking at the scabs, not letting them heal. In his head, the only thing that was going to make any difference was getting to meet Mr Brill. Sit down with him, look him in the eye and ask why he'd done it. What had made *him* so special? Because, at the moment, that was the last thing he felt. He had to get out of this house . . .

'But you can't go just yet, Seb! I don't know what . . . '

'I phoned the doctor, Mum . . . he said, as long as I took it easy, I'd be fine.' Seb walked over to his mum, who had turned her back to him and was standing by the sink, fiddling with the kettle. 'I'll be fine, Mum . . . and I've got to get out the house, it's driving me bloody mad being stuck in here.'

'I'll be worried . . . '

'Don't, Mum, it won't help.' Seb reached out and patted her shoulder. 'Sooner or later . . . '

Before he could finish, his mum had turned round and was hugging him and sobbing. It was so unexpected he had no idea what to do.

'I can't stay in the house for the rest of my life, Mum . . . '

'I'm sorry,' she sniffed, looking away, embarrassed, and letting him go. 'Don't know what came over me . . . your brother not here . . . you looking like you were about to die . . . couldn't bear it.'

'But I'm fine now, and Tony'll be back, he won't be able to stand all that Florida sunshine for ever!'

'Promise me something?'

'What?'

'Don't turn it off . . . when you're out . . . don't ever turn it off . . . '

Freedom beckoned and it felt, on the one hand, great. And on the other . . . on the other he was sick with nervousness, with a hollow feeling in the pit of his stomach and a total craving for cigarettes. He'd been planning this moment almost since he'd come home, over three weeks ago, and now that he was being allowed out he found himself looking for excuses not to go.

Like, had he done all the background work he needed to on Jay Brill? Did he really *need* to go back up west? Was he *really* totally OK, you know, physically? Would that bastard Zack see him and have another go? What had happened to the psycho who'd nearly killed him? And what about the girl?

Each time he came up with a reason to stay at home, safe, another part of his head delivered an answer as to why he should get up off his backside and get on with it.

For starters, during the last few days he'd researched the hell out of Mr Bloody Brill; it wasn't, to his great surprise, as unusual a surname as he'd thought it would be, and there were quite a few in the phonebook. Only there were no J. Brills. He'd gone on the Web to have a look as well. There he'd found a whole page of Jay Brills, but none of them fitted the profile – they were either too old, or they were just not the sort of person to be hanging round the Embankment at 2am, or they didn't live in England. Most of them, if not all, lived in America.

And then, if he wasn't strong enough by now, he never would be; he was also going to be keeping a weather eye out for Zack, and if he saw him he was sprinting. Plus, even if he saw the psycho again – which he really seriously doubted – the state each of them had been in meant it was unlikely they'd be able to recognise one another . . . and the girl?

It occurred to him that he'd hardly thought about Janey – if that really was her name – at all since that night, but thinking about her now was like watching a short, very-badly shot video clip that only lasted about ten minutes, from walking into her room to walking out again. He found it hard to work out why, of everything he'd done that day, he'd done that. It wasn't as if he'd been desperately trying to lose his virginity or anything. He'd been pissed – but not pissed enough to make him incapable of performing – and, now that he was stone-cold sober, he supposed it must've seemed like the logical thing to do at the time.

He certainly remembered what Janey looked like, but doubted she'd remember just another lagered-up customer. So, no excuses. He had to go.

* * *

'Hi, Dad . . . '

'Seb?'

'Mum made me promise to call you, once I got to the West End.'

'Right . . . '

'So, I'm here.'

'Fine . . . be careful . . . she does worry.'

'See you tonight, Dad.'

It was weird how different everything looked in the daylight. He couldn't say he'd been paying much attention the last time he was there; he'd been cold, hungry and aching all over, so the details of his surroundings hadn't really sunk in that fateful night.

With the sun doing its best to shine through the thin cloud cover, the area around Embankment station – the small park, the posh hotel, the wide sweep of Villiers Street taking you down to the tube, beyond it the road and the Thames – looked so totally unlike it did at night it could almost be in an alternate universe. One where tramps and derelicts, down-and-outs and lost boys didn't exist.

Fact was, but for a sole *Big Issue* seller and his dog, everyone looked like they had a nice home to go to and wouldn't, in a million years, queue up at some van for a cup of vegetable soup. There was no soup van either.

'S'cuse me . . . '

'It's a pound-twenty, mate.' The man – Seb could see from his badge that he was *Big Issue* seller number 471265 – held out a magazine.

'Oh . . . right . . . ' Seb dug out a couple of coins and

took the mag. 'Uh, d'you know where I could find the soup van that parks out here at night?'

'Don't do nights, sunshine,' said the man. 'No point, all the money's gone home t'bed.'

'D'you know the one I mean, though?'

'A soup van's a soup van . . . you get 'em all over.'

'This one was run by a couple of blokes, they had short hair, you know like shaved heads, and one of them had these big silver earrings in each ear.'

'If they had the wottsits, the paint on their foreheads, then it was prob'ly the Hare-fuckin'-Krishnas.' The man made a pained face. 'Drive you nuts, banging their bloody drums and clanking their little cymbals all bloody day . . . 'swhy I left me Oxford Street pitch . . . couldn't bloody stand it any more.'

'Right . . . but d'you know where the soup vans go back to?'

'Not a clue, mate,' said the man, handing over a magazine to another passer-by and pocketing the money, 'but if I ever see one again, I'm gonna bang on the side of it with a dustbin lid for an hour solid an' see how much they like it.'

Seb didn't remember specifically seeing anything to do with the Hare Krishnas on the van, but figured the *Big Issue* seller was more up to speed on soup vans than he was and started asking around. The bloke at the paper stand didn't know anything, the guy selling sweets and fags just shook his head, and the woman running the flower stall gave him a lecture about getting involved with cults. It was one of the staff at the tube station who finally suggested, a bit sarcastically, that he'd find where they were in the phone-book. Obvious, really. And there, stuck between *Hare in the Gate* and *Hare Nicholas, Archts,* was the Hare Krishna Temple, Soho Square. He set off.

The route he followed took him through Covent Garden, across Cambridge Circus and into Soho via Old Compton Street. Each phone box he passed on the way was covered in tart cards and in almost every one he saw Crazy Janey's face staring out at him. It was like he was being shadowed. It freaked him and made him feel exposed and vulnerable, like Zack could be anywhere, watching and waiting.

Odd thing was, although the streets were so full it was like wading through a flood of people, Seb still felt isolated and alone. Defenceless. What must it be like to feel like this and not have a home to go to?

It was a relief when he finally walked into Soho Square from Greek Street. It was lunchtime and the sight of all the people eating their sandwiches in one of those odd little places in which London seems to specialise – a small, fenced-off park, complete with a Tudor-style house in the middle – made him feel hungry. He walked round the square, and as he came to the north side he looked for the Hare Krishna temple. Nothing looked much like a temple, but as he got nearer he saw that the ground-floor place next to a pub was a restaurant. Govinda's. All you could eat for £4.99, if you were prepared to go veggie. How bad could it be? Seb went in to find out.

The place was busy and, from the look of the people serving, it had to have something to do with the Krishnas. But, as no one looked like they'd time to chat right then, Seb got some food and decided to wait until the lunch crowd had disappeared. After he'd finished his food, which he was surprised to find was better than OK, and flicked through the *Big Issue*, he'd grabbed a couple of pamphlets from a nearby dispenser and was idly glancing at them when someone sat down opposite him.

'Hare Krishna . . . would you like to know some more about us?'

'Sorry?' Seb looked up to see a young woman smiling at him from across the table.

'I saw you reading the literature,' said the woman, 'and I thought I could help explain anything you weren't sure of.'

Seb looked at her; she was obviously English – pale skin, mousy-brown hair, light blue eyes, nondescript features – but she was dressed in a sari, like an Indian woman, and had the two lines of light-coloured paint drawn down her forehead that the *Big Issue* seller had mentioned. It was like looking at one of those videos where they morph the face, mixing and matching. She didn't look or sound quite right.

'No, I'm fine,' he said, and the woman smiled again and began to get up. 'Although I do need some information . . . '

The woman sat down again.

'I need to find a soup van,' said Seb, 'and I think it might be one of yours – you do have soup vans, don't you?'

'We call it "Food For Life", it's more than just soup,' she said. 'Why do you want to find one?'

'I . . . ' Seb stopped. How could he explain why he wanted to find the van without going into more detail than he really wanted to?

'Yes?'

'Oh, right, well . . . it's like this . . . ' He looked at her bland, open face smiling questioningly at him, and couldn't bring himself to make up some elaborate lie that would cover up the truth like earth on a coffin. 'I was beaten up by a guy, down by Embankment tube station, and some other guy fundamentally waded in and, like saved my life. Basically.'

'Oh.'

'And I wanted to find him and say thanks,' Seb went on, 'but I don't know who he is or where he lives or anything.'

'I see . . . '

'There was a van there – it was late, like two in the morning – and I think it might have been one of yours,' he went on, finding that explaining things to a total stranger wasn't at all difficult. 'The two guys running it must've seen everything and I just need to talk to them.'

'Right.'

'Do you know where I could find them?'

'No.'

'No?'

'I don't, but someone else might be able to help,' said the woman, getting up and walking away without another word.

Seb watched her cross the restaurant, the material of her sari swinging left and right as she walked, a movement echoed by her long, thin pigtail. She made her way through the tables to the back of the restaurant where he saw her start talking to a man. He had a shaved head and was dressed in a shapeless white top and baggy white trousers; she was pointing over at him as she spoke. Seb felt like he was in the middle of some weird spy movie, and the feeling of being watched folded over him like a black cloth.

He surreptitiously checked behind him, looking to see if anyone really was watching. In a spy movie you could tell because the bad guys were always so obviously crap, hiding behind newspapers and stuff, but he had an idea that in real life it would be very different.

No one was even glancing his way, and Seb began to

wonder if he was taking this being careful thing just a bit too far, like by getting paranoid about it. How the hell did you know if you were paranoid or not anyway? He didn't *think* he was, but *if* he was he wouldn't think he was, would he. All he did know was that thinking this kind of shit for long enough would definitely send you over the edge . . .

CHAPTER 6

FINALLY THE MAN WITH THE SHAVED HEAD stopped talking to the girl, and he turned and started to walk across the restaurant towards Seb. He wasn't smiling, he wasn't frowning, and from a distance his face was expressionless and weirdly blank. Almost like a robot. As he got nearer, Seb could see that he was just very calm. Calm and sort of perfect, in a bland kind of way.

'Hare Krishna,' he said, sitting down opposite him. 'How can I help you?'

'Did she tell you?' Seb nodded across the restaurant to where the girl was still standing. 'About the van? I need to find it.'

'I'm sorry to hear about what happened to you . . . are you better now?'

'Yeah . . . yeah, much better, thanks . . . '

'One of our vans does go near to Embankment station,' the man said. He wasn't Indian either, he had the palest skin and the bluest eyes Seb had ever seen, which only added to his air of strange perfection. The only thing that let him down, he noticed, were his teeth, which were irregular and slightly grey. He looked at Seb as if expecting an answer.

'Right . . . '

'But not at night. Are you trying to catch the man who attacked you?'

'No . . . ' Seb looked over at the girl. What had she told him? 'No, they got him, he's been put away somewhere – I want to find the man who pulled him off me, saved my life . . . the people in the van would've seen everything, and I thought they might be able to help me find him. So I could say thanks.'

'OK . . . '

Seb waited. The man looked away and appeared to frown slightly.

'Is that all right?'

'I think it's a very good idea.'

'Great . . . so, like, do you know who would've been there that night? You know, if it wasn't your people?'

'How long ago did this happen?'

'About a month.' Seb frowned to himself as he thought of all the lost days. 'Yeah . . . four weeks.'

'We'll have to go next door.'

'Next door?'

'To the temple, to find out who you want to speak to.'

You got into the temple by going to the small shopfront next door to the restaurant and up the stairs to the first floor. It was just a room, decorated in a sort of iced-cake, Bollywood style, with gaudy pictures all over the walls and some square cushions on the floor. Seb sat on a bench in the corridor, next to a man in a business suit who was muttering, 'Hare Krishna, Hare Krishna . . . ' under his breath, and waited.

Five minutes later the man came out of the temple, and Seb stood as he put his shoes back on and walked over to him. 'Ravi says there's another group of people who do the night run.' He looked back into the temple and Seb saw someone looking at them, smiling. 'He says two of their volunteers work up in Kentish Town, at the Job Centre.'

The thought occurred to Seb as he came out of the tube that, even with the sun shining, Kentish Town High Street still looked sorry for itself. It looked a bit better than it usually did when he and his mates walked home through it after the Camden Town clubs closed, but not by much.

He knew where the Job Centre was, some way along the High Street, down from the station, and when he saw it he almost turned round and went straight home. It was like the worst kind of waking nightmare; a couple of street people were hanging around outside, sharing a can of Tennent's Super, and a girl, no older than him, was coming out pushing a buggy with a young kid in it. It was an advert for where you really didn't ever want to be. He felt the hairs on the back of his neck go up and a shiver run down his spine. He waited for a second or two, took a deep breath and went in.

He saw a guy with a shaved head at the back of the room. It was hard to tell from a distance if he had earrings, but there was definitely something familiar about him. The man noticed Seb staring and was walking towards him before he'd worked out what to say.

'Can I help you?'

Seb felt like it was the first piece of good luck he'd had. The two guys had been running the soup van that night. And they'd witnessed the whole thing. Tom, the one with earrings, had listened to him, then gone off to get his mate,

Chris, and they'd taken him off to a nearby caff to talk. It was only when they ordered him a strong cup of coffee and sat him down that he realised he was quite shaken. These were people who'd seen what happened to him.

'You OK?' Tom looked concerned. 'We asked around, man, but no one knew anything.'

Chris frowned. 'Except that the bloke who attacked you got sectioned and taken off somewhere.'

'D'you mind if I smoke?' Seb stirred his coffee again and again. 'I'm sort of giving up, but I kind of wouldn't mind one right now . . . '

Tom and Chris nodded, Tom reaching over to the next table and picking up an ashtray. 'Feel free, it's a caff, mate.'

'So, did you see everything that happened?'

'Pretty much, didn't we, Chris?' Tom took Seb's box of matches, struck one and offered it to him.

'Yeah, but it all happened so fast.' Chris shook his head. 'I remember that guy pushing you out of the way . . . we'd seen him before, right? Knew he was trouble . . . everyone tried to keep clear of him, and I s'pose it should've been obvious he was going to hurt someone, sooner or later.'

'Thing is, no one wants to take responsibility for people like him.' Tom blew the match out and put it back in the box, pushing the tray backwards and forwards, in and out. 'They want them to fall off the edge, disappear.'

'At least you feed 'em.'

'Small comfort.' Chris shook his head again, half smiling.

'What happened when he attacked me?'

'It all kicked off when your phone went, didn't it?' Seb nodded. 'That made me and Tom look over . . . you don't hear mobiles much around the van at that time of the morning . . . I just saw him beating the living shit out of you.'

'It was like slow-motion, man.' Tom was still fiddling with the matchbox.

'D'you want a fag?' Seb offered him his packet.

'No, thanks. Given up.'

'Why'd he lose it like that?' Seb tapped ash off his cigarette.

'Who knows . . . ' Tom shrugged. 'You don't look for logic out there.'

'What happened then?'

'Then this other guy came out of the dark and just laid into him, never seen anything like it.' Chris looked at Tom, who nodded in agreement. 'All the other guys were keeping well out of it, but he went straight in . . . by the time we'd got out the van, he'd pulled him off you and had him face down in the gutter, kneeling on his back.'

'He told us to take over holding the bloke – took the two of us and a couple of the others to keep him there, he was mad as a pig.'

'And the guy?'

'He went over to you,' Chris pointed at Seb. 'Took his coat off and covered you . . . yelling for someone to call an ambulance . . . I was kind of amazed there was anyone left there to do it, tell the truth; everyone normally runs at the first sign of trouble.'

'Police got there first, though – a Panda car.' Tom started opening and closing the box of matches again. 'They cuffed him and had him in the back of their car by the time the ambulance turned up . . . I think they stayed around to see if you were still alive . . . you know, was it just going to be an assault charge, or something more serious.'

'That's when everyone legged it,' Chris took the matchbox away from Tom, 'you know, when they realised names and addresses might be taken?'

Seb had one of those moments which, if he'd been a cartoon character, would have ended up with him having a lightbulb over his head. 'Did they take Jay's – the man's name and details?'

'Couldn't say, I didn't notice.' Chris put the matchbox over on Seb's side of the faded, scratched Formica table.

'Me neither.'

Seb's shoulders slumped.

'Could be wrong.' Tom reached over and picked up the matches again. 'You'll have to, like, ask the cops won't you . . . '

It hadn't occurred to Seb that he should talk to the police. He always felt slightly uneasy around them, and had been stopped and searched one time too many to ever think of them as being on his side.

'Yeah, I will . . . so what was this bloke like, then?'

Both Chris and Tom looked at each other. 'Sort of, like, *ordinary*,' Tom shrugged again, 'brown hair, about 5'10"ish, nothing special, really . . . off-the-peg sort of person.'

'Except for the wossnames,' Chris circled a finger over his forearm, 'you know, his tattoos.'

'Right!' Tom nodded. 'On his arms.'

'What about them?'

'They were odd, not like the stuff you normally see.' Tom leant forward, elbow on the table, cupping his chin with his hand. 'They were squiggles, like just black graphics, not a picture or anything.'

'Can you draw them for me?' Seb grabbed a serviette and searched in his backpack for a ballpoint.

'Got one.' Tom reached into his pocket for a pen, picked up the serviette and spread it out. 'He had one about halfway down each forearm . . . lemme see . . . '

It took him a number of goes, with help from Chris, but some minutes later Seb found himself staring at two roughly-sketched symbols:

$$\alpha \qquad \zeta$$

'The one that looked like half an infinity sign was on his right arm – right, Chris? And the other one, the snakey one, that was on his left arm.' Tom pointed at Seb's arms with the ballpoint. 'Saw 'em cos he'd, you know, like I said, taken his coat off and his sleeves were rolled up.'

'What do they mean?' asked Seb.

'Dunno,' Tom shook his head. 'Chris?'

'No idea.'

'Can I keep this?' Seb picked up the serviette.

'Course . . . what're you going to do now?' Tom wadded up all the other sketches and then began picking the ball of paper apart.

'Are you going to the police?' Chris's question hung in the air, waiting to be answered.

'Rather not . . . '

'What's the alternative?' Tom didn't look at him, just carried on picking away at the ball of paper.

'Try and find one of the other people there, see if they know anything about the guy.' Seb put the serviette in his backpack. 'Someone out there must know *something* . . . '

'You be careful.' Chris looked concerned. 'They don't trust people, specially people who go round asking questions.'

'Any idea where I could go?'

Tom looked up. 'There's a couple of spikes off Drury Lane.'

'Spikes?'

'Hostels.' Tom now had a small pile of shredded serviette paper in front of him.

'Right . . . ' Seb looked at his watch as he pushed his chair back, thinking that Tom was probably the kind of person who really wished he hadn't given up smoking. He wondered if he'd ever manage to properly do it himself. 'I'll go down there tomorrow.'

'Good to meet you.' Tom got up with him.

'Thanks for all your help.'

'No trouble . . . sorry we couldn't remember any more.' Tom put his hand out and Seb shook it.

'Easy,' Chris nodded, 'be lucky.'

As Seb stood on the platform, waiting for the train, he found himself drawn to the tube map. He'd always liked it, fascinated by the way whoever had designed it had made everything so neat. His dad had once showed him how it bore no relation at all to reality, the position of the stations on the coloured lines having nothing at all to do with where the places were on an actual map. It was a graphic dream. Someone's attempt to make the world work the way they'd wanted. And it did work. It was like an instruction manual for the whole of London, which in its original form had been perfect. It was spoiled now, with the jagged grey slabs of the different zones messing things up, but, if you half-closed your eyes, you could almost get rid of them.

Things would be so much easier if they always worked to a pattern. Why, he thought, like with the zones on the tube map design, were people always doing things that messed stuff up? And then there were people like Jay Brill, who appeared at the most extraordinary moments to make things better. Why?

CHAPTER 7

GOING BACK UP WEST FOR THE SECOND TIME WAS easier – now that he'd done it once and survived. This time, though, he'd be talking to people who didn't necessarily want to talk to him, people who might get stressed out and unreasonable, if he pushed it. Today, he told himself as he walked up the escalator at Leicester Square station, he was going to have to practise extreme caution.

Even with that thought kind of pinned right up front in his mind, where he couldn't miss it, he still went the long way round to Drury Lane. The way that took him past the building with the scuffed door where Crazy Janey worked. Nothing like tempting Fate.

He stood and looked at the building from the opposite side of the street, staring up at the top floor windows on the right of the building, wondering what the hell he'd been doing going in there. Wondering who was up there now. He was scared shitless Zack would catch him and, at the same time, magnetically drawn to the place, but in the end fear won out and he carried on walking.

'Seb?'

  'Yeah?'

  'Where are you?'

'Up west.'

'Again? You were up there yesterday . . . '

'I'm researching, Mum, for my art project . . . like I told you.'

'Will you be late?'

'Depends what you call late.'

'You'll be back for supper?'

'Course.'

'Just be careful . . . '

'Mum!'

Maybe it was because of what had happened to him, but Seb was far more aware of the street now. The part of it that kind of remains invisible, if you ignore it. The part of the street that slinks out of the way when you look directly at it, or else follows you, sniffing hungrily at your heels.

It was the frayed edge of the world he knew, inhabited by the long-time drunks – their bottle-scarred faces, tanned like leather, and their unmistakable perfume of piss and sweat and beer – and the junkies, strung-out crack and speed freaks, and chemical cowboys, all thin as scarecrows, pale eyes skittering in a frantic search for a lifeline. Even in bright daylight they were ghosts, detached but with their own oppressive, overriding concerns. An alternate reality that was only vaguely in touch with his.

Where they were was just one step over the border. An easy trip to make. You could do it without even meaning to, without even thinking. Seb still had the scars of his visit. He sat down on the steps of a building and lit a cigarette, watching. With his street eyes peeled he saw the stuff going on that most people preferred to turn a blind eye to. He didn't want to go back there. He didn't want to make contact again, but he knew he had to if he was ever to have a chance of finding Jay Brill, and maybe get some answers.

The first time he'd got close to the edge was when he'd started buying his dope and the occasional pill or tab from some friend of a friend who'd lived in a scuzzy bedsit over in Finsbury Park. Those furtive visits to Jon the Hat, as he liked to be called, had been kind of exciting, as there was always an outside chance of being stopped and searched. It had happened, but they'd been lucky and never been caught carrying. And Jon wasn't a serious dealer, either, just some mildly spaced geezer who did a bit of business on the side.

But Jon was also his introduction to Martin. Thanks, Jon. And that's when the edge got a lot nearer. It occurred to Seb that he and his mates had really been just a bunch of soft boys, playing at being bad. True bad was dangerous. Truly bad people had no rules and played for keeps. Martin wasn't evil, he had rules, but what he plainly didn't have was any morals. Seb wasn't sure if he actually knew what evil really was, like the guy who put him in hospital wasn't evil, he was plainly fucked in the head, but not evil. Maybe, to be evil, you had to plan the excessively bad things you did and then enjoy the hell out of it when you did them.

What he did know was, he was pretty sure he'd never met anyone you could accurately call a real evil person. Probably not even close. But what was also pretty obvious was that a truly good person had done him the favour of saving his life. Though would he ever meet him?

'Oi!'

Seb looked over his shoulder to see some fat bloke in a toy-cop uniform pointing at him. He looked away. Doormen. What a sad bunch of petty tyrants they usually were. Always shooing you away from their patch when you dared get too close, squeezing that last bit of Little Hitler power out of their position.

'You there!'

Seb stubbed his cigarette out on the step, stood up and began to walk away.

'You clear that up,' said the man, moving in front of him. 'This place isn't a bloody ashtray, you know!'

Seb looked at him. He was short, which made him look even fatter, and he had a thin, sandy moustache clinging for dear life to his upper lip. He stared, frowning aggressively at Seb, his tiny, dark brown eyes squinted, his small mouth pursed, and Seb could smell his aftershave, a wave of its overly sweet, flowery smell coating the inside of his nose. The man stood, hovering, just out of reach.

'What?'

'I said pick that up.' The man pointed down, as if Seb might have not seen what he'd done. He had a couple of biros in the pocket of his light blue shirt, a mobile in a scuffed leather case attached to his belt on one side and a thick chain clipped to his belt loop on the other side and running into his bulging trouser pocket. Keys, thought Seb. The symbols of his power.

It could be a laugh, winding up these guys, but he didn't feel like doing it today. And he also didn't feel like kowtowing to this small-minded jobsworth.

'Fuck off.' Seb turned away and as he did so he noticed some people walking through the foyer of the building towards them; out of the corner of his eye, he saw the security man walk back up the steps.

'Morning, Ms Hawkins . . . '

Ms *Hawkins*? Seb looked over at the group of people,

three women and two men. Sure enough, one of the women was the person he'd stolen the wallet from, what was her name? Sara? She seemed to be the centre of the group, the planet around which the others all orbited. No surprises there, then, as she'd sounded like she was the ego from Hell when she'd sat next to him on the bench outside the supermarket.

'. . . Just clearing squatters off the front steps, ma'am . . . use the place like it was public property, don't they.'

'Is that my cab down there, George?' Sara Hawkins ignored what he'd said and looked at her watch.

'Yes, it's . . . '

'We're going to be late.' She turned away from him as he spoke. 'Molly, call ahead and let them know.'

Seb watched as Sara Hawkins led three of the people away to a waiting black people-carrier, leaving Molly and George standing on the steps.

'A "please" would be nice, once in a while, you know what I mean, George?' Molly looked like she'd smelled something that'd died.

'Yeah, well, she always treats me OK, you know, like at Christmas.' George checked his fingernails. 'Sees me right.'

'She treats you like a flunkey, George, and you know it.' Molly looked over at Seb, who was standing, watching them. 'She wouldn't piss on you if you were on fire,' Molly told him, then walked stiffly back into the office.

'She's got no respect, that one . . . ' George, who'd developed a very visible nervous twitch in his left eye, then turned on him. 'And don't let me catch *you* around here again, either.'

Seb looked at the name etched into one of the glass panels surrounding the foyer entrance as he flicked his fag-end at the gutter. The AMH Agency. Whatever that was.

'Bye, George,' he said, as he walked off. 'Don't catch on fire . . . '

Seb felt sorry for Molly. He had no idea what she was like as a person, but liked to think she didn't deserve to be treated by her boss the way he'd witnessed Sara Hawkins do now on two occasions. George, on the other hand, was a weasel. And Ms Hawkins was not a nice person. Not that that made stealing from her a good thing to do, but Seb couldn't help it, the fact that she was a right royal bitch-for-all-seasons did make him feel less guilty as he walked away from the building.

Guilt. What a weird trip that was. And if anyone had a lot to feel guilty about, he did. Thing was, it wasn't as if he was denying anything he'd done, or claiming none of it was his fault. He just had things to get on with that feeling guilty wouldn't help.

Sometimes, life really could be that simple.

Five minutes later he found himself at the top of Drury Lane. Down which he had to go to find people who might have been witnesses to his life being saved. He stood looking along the street; it was one-way, the traffic coming up towards him and the pavements on both sides pretty full of people. It wasn't going to be hard to spot the types he'd have to talk to, but exactly how to start the conversation was something else entirely.

'S'cuse me . . . '
  'Fuck off.'
  'OK. Sure. It's just that . . . '

'I said . . . '
'Fine, OK . . . '

Seb lost count of the times that scenario, or something remarkably similar, had happened. The couple of times he'd actually managed to get past the initial hostility, he'd been conned into buying cans of Tennent's Super, and then told to fuck off.

Like Tom and Chris had said, there were two spikes off Drury Lane, neither of which allowed people to stay in them all day, so there were plenty of people to choose to talk to. Trouble was, in a close and closed community like theirs, Seb discovered that word soon got around. And the word seemed to be that there was this limp kid on the street asking questions, and if you were lucky enough, you got a free beer.

'S'cuse me?'
  'What?'
  'You the geezer askin' questions?'
  'Yeah.'
  'Gimme a beer an' ask me anything you like.'
  'Fuck off.'

The attitude was catching. And so was the feeling of hopelessness these people carried with them. It was in their dirty, piss-stained clothes, their broken-toothed smiles, their mahogany fingers. When you were this far down, was the unspoken message, there was no possible way out. This was it. Seb found it amazing that despair didn't just shut them down for good, turn off the will to live. Whatever it was that kept a person's spirit alight, even when it might seem to an observer like a completely pointless thing to do, that thing must be one seriously tough bastard.

At some point, after one more futile attempt to make contact with someone – end result: being spat at – Seb went into the supermarket down towards the theatre, bought himself a sandwich and went to sit on the bench outside. The bench where this whole thing had sort of started.

He was just a little phased by the almost Groundhog Day feeling he got, being where he was. Like at any moment it could begin all over again and there would be nothing he could do to stop himself going on the same downhill race as before, and maybe this time there wouldn't be someone to haul him back from oblivion.

This whole train of thought spaced him out, made him feel totally disconnected. Staring off into the middle distance, eyes focused on nothing in particular, hand feeding the sandwich to his mouth like his body was running a program, he was only half aware of someone sitting down next to him. Realising that he was being observed, he turned and looked at who had joined him.

'You the bloke asking questions?'

'Uh, yes . . . '

'Gather you're not having much luck.'

'You could say that.'

'Something about a fight, was it? A couple of weeks or so ago?'

'Bit more than that, but yes . . . why? D'you know something?'

'Yeah.'

'What d'you want . . . beer?'

'I could be insulted by that, you know.'

'Sorry, it's just that . . . '

'I know, experience has taught you . . . if you could front some egg and chips, instead of a beer, there's a caff just up the street.'

HE WASN'T LIKE THE OTHERS, NOW SEB CAME TO look at him more closely. The bloke sitting opposite him was obviously down, but no way was he out. For a start, he didn't have that dull, stunned look in his eyes that Seb had come to recognise as a major shutdown syndrome. His name was Billy, he said, Billy Swift from the West Country, and he'd been travelling for ten years. No particular place to go, nothing and no one to tie him down, he said.

It was hard to tell how old Billy was, with his stubbled face and ragged haircut. He smiled a lot, though, showing crow's feet round his eyes and a couple of missing teeth, and he had surprisingly delicate hands with badly bitten nails. He could have been anything, thought Seb, from late twenties to late thirties, the life he led. The one thing that seemed clear was that he didn't appear to be a career alky or into serious drugs in a big enough way to have done any permanent damage.

Seb watched Billy as he worked his way through the egg, beans, chips, two toasts and a tea he'd bought him. He'd got himself a tea as well, but no food as he'd just had the sandwich and wasn't hungry, and waited until Billy had finished and was wiping his plate with the last of his toast before lighting up.

'You remember that night then?'

'Clear as day.'

'So . . . um . . . what did you see?'

Billy sat back, took a crumpled Benson's pack out of his jacket pocket and fished up a pinched-out dog-end.

'Save it.' Seb pushed his packet across the table.

'Thanks,' Billy smiled, taking one of Seb's Marlboros and lighting it with one of his own matches, which he flicked out with his thumb in a practised move he must've done thousands of times it was so slick. 'A piece of advice, if you're going to be round here much more . . . generosity's often seen as a weakness . . . a fool and his money, as they say.'

'I've noticed.'

'I bet you have.'

'That night then . . . '

'I turned up after you . . . saw you walk off from the van, looking like something the cat'd dragged in. And then that mad bastard came along. Always a sign of trouble on the horizon, those ones.'

'Why d'you hang around?'

'Didn't think it'd kick off that quickly, to be honest . . . it was that bloody phone of yours did it.'

'Don't remind me, I had to change the ringtone, cos every time I got a call I got a flashback to that nutter kicking the shit out of me.'

'You still got the same phone – it didn't get trashed?'

'Came out of that whole thing looking a whole lot better than I did.'

'Never had one, me.' Billy stubbed his fag out, smiling to himself. 'When you think about it, it's people like us should have mobiles, wouldn't you say? Not having a home to have a phone in?'

'Yeah, right.' Seb nodded distractedly. 'And the man who saved me . . . d'you know, like where I can find him?'

'Couldn't tell you.'

'What?'

'Never seen him before, he wasn't a regular, not one of the ones you see around all the time.'

Seb, who'd been staring at Billy, looked away, suddenly feeling completely empty. Gutted. Like there was no point any more, no fucking point at all, and that he'd just been conned, again. This time by a real pro. He leant over the table, picked up his fags and pushed back his chair.

'You off?'

'Not much point hanging round here . . . you got what you wanted and there's nothing for me.' Seb stood up, angry at himself for being dicked about. 'You probably weren't even there, were you? You just made the whole fucking thing up, didn't you, eh?' Billy wasn't smiling now, he just sat at the table looking up at Seb. 'Why's it so difficult to get an honest answer out of anybody? Why's everyone try to rip you off the whole time?'

Billy lit his pinched-out dog-end, still watching Seb, still saying nothing.

'All I want to do is find some bloke and say thank you for saving my fucking life, and all I get is messed around.'

'And you think *I'm* messing you round?'

'Yeah.'

'Cos I don't know some geezer's name?'

'Uh, yeah?'

'Like, because I'm out here I'm supposed to know *every* fucking person out here too? You think this is some nice, cosy club, don't you? Where we all stick together and look

72

out for each other . . . that all for one and one for all crap?'

It was Seb's turn to be silent.

'Just sit your baggy, middle-class arse down and stop feeling so sorry for yourself.'

Seb did as he was told.

'You gotta remember, the normal rules don't apply in this neck of the woods, cos no one gives a shit about outsiders. And who the fuck are you to come poking your nose into where you're not wanted? What makes *you* think you can walk out your nice house in the morning to come slumming it for a while, for as long as you need to get what you want – where'd you get that idea from?'

'I'm sorry, OK?' Seb took out a cigarette and offered the pack to Billy. 'And don't take this offer the wrong way, either.'

'I won't.' Billy took a fag. 'But if anyone should know how dangerous it is at street level, you should. And I *am* trying to help.'

'D'you want another cup of tea?'

'I'll get 'em.'

Seb watched Billy go over to the counter and talk to the girl behind it. He felt completely confused. If this guy Billy didn't know anything about Jay Brill, what was the point in staying? He'd be better off cutting his losses and going back out, a little wiser than before, to see what he could find elsewhere.

'I got us a slice of fruit cake each as well.'

'Thanks . . . you didn't have to.'

'I know.' Billy sat down. 'Tea'll be over in a minute.'

'Sorry for going off on one.'

'I wouldn't still be sitting here if I didn't realise that.'

'What'm I gonna do now? D'you think there's *anyone* out

there who's going to know where I can find this guy?'

'Could be.'

'A light somewhere at the end of the tunnel, then?'

'Look, you've as much chance of seeing the guy walking around, bumping into him on the street, as you have of finding someone who knows where he is . . . have you been to the police yet?'

'No.'

Billy gave him a questioning look.

'Last resort . . . I'd rather do it myself.'

'You got any paper, biro or a pen and stuff?'

'Got a sketchpad and some pencils.' They were part of his art project excuse for being up west.

'Can I have a borrow?'

'Yeah . . . ' Seb dug into his backpack and brought out an A5 Daler pad and grey metal pencil case, handing them over to Billy. 'What're you going to do?'

'I remember what he looks like . . . gonna do you a sketch, like on TV. OK?'

Seb nodded, watching as Billy turned the pad to a clean page and picked out a 2B and an HB pencil from the case. He had no idea what to expect, but as soon as he saw the first dark grey marks on the off-white paper, he knew Billy had done this before.

'Where d'you learn to draw?'

'Always could . . . it's what I liked doing most.'

'Did you go to art school?'

'For a bit . . . it got boring after a while, so I left.'

Seb could see an upside-down face appearing on the pad, Billy drawing in quick, clean lines and never stopping to rub anything out, only pausing to change pencils once or twice. His art teacher had told him about people with something called an eidetic memory; they had a mind like a camera and were able to remember everything they'd seen and reproduce it exactly the way it was. Seb thought maybe Billy was like this, the way he was drawing.

'Can I look?'

'Sure.'

The right way up the sketch was even more impressive. Jay Brill now had a face. In the three-quarter view Billy had drawn he looked to be in his late 20s, early 30s, with longish hair, dark eyes and a small gold hoop earring. He had quite a prominent nose and a squareish jaw and looked straight off the paper at him. Seb felt sure he'd have no trouble recognising that face, if he ever saw it again.

'You're pretty good, you know?'

'It's no big deal.'

'That's what he looks like?'

'That's what he looks like.'

'And you only saw him the once, right?'

'Yeah . . . '

Seb picked up the sketchpad and looked at it more closely. There wasn't a single line wasted in the drawing, every mark on the paper was essential to telling the Jay Brill story. 'Would you sign this?'

'What for?' Billy lit a match and watched it slowly burn out, dropping it in the ashtray just before the yellow-blue flame reached his finger and thumb. 'Cos one day I might be famous? I don't think so . . . someone did once say I could make a good bit of cash doing the tourist thing down Leicester Square, but I couldn't take the hassle of making fat Yanks look prettier than they deserved to be – know what I mean?'

'There's other ways, right? I mean, you've got real talent, man . . . '

'There's a quote I remember.' Billy frowned as he thought. 'Flattery's like smoking – it's all right so long as you don't inhale ... which reminds me, can I thieve another of your fags?'

As Seb handed over the packet he tried to get his head round Billy Swift. He was, what was it called? An anomaly? Something like that. Hard to figure out, anyway. Why would anyone who could do something as good as he could choose to waste it, throw it away like it was a worthless piece of litter? Maybe cos he did see it as worthless.

'Go on,' Seb tapped the pad, 'sign it ... '

'Wanna know something else I read somewhere?' Billy picked up a pencil and carefully wrote his name and the date at the bottom of the drawing.

'What?'

'You shouldn't ever regret what you do, only what you *don't* do ... can't remember who said it, but they sure as fuck knew what they were talking about.'

'I'll remember that.' Seb took the pad and the pencils and put everything back in his bag.

'It's been nice to meet you, Seb.' Billy reached out his hand.

Seb leant over and shook it. 'See you.'

'Stranger things have happened.'

'Thanks for the drawing.'

'Watch out for yourself.' Billy moved his hand in a slow arc in front of him.

'You too.'

It was some minutes later that Seb realised he was just walking, with no thought to where he was actually going, not really looking where he'd been. For all he knew, he could've walked right past Jay Brill and never noticed.

CHAPTER 9

N HIS BEDROOM, TAKING UP ALMOST HALF OF ONE wall, Seb had a large pinboard. His dad had made it for him, sticking cork tiles to a piece of hardboard and finishing it off with a simple frame. As soon as Seb'd got back from the West End, he'd cleared a couple of tiles' worth of space on it and pinned up a photostat of Billy Swift's drawing and another of the tattoo symbols Tom and Chris had given him.

It was weird, but now, wherever you were in the room, Jay Brill's eyes followed you. Which was really quite cool, so Seb sat in his beanbag chair and stared back at the drawing, wondering what the hell the symbols he had on his arms meant, and cursing himself for forgetting to ask Billy if he'd seen them and, if he had, whether he had any idea what they were about.

Jay Brill now had a face, and Seb wondered if finding out what the strange symbols meant would give him anything that would help in actually finding the man. Apart from going back out and repeating what he'd done the day before – which, except for meeting Billy, boiled down to getting the piss taken out of him – the only option he really had left was going to the police. And loath though he was to do it, he couldn't see any other way of getting any further; if he smartened up and asked nicely, he supposed he

wouldn't be hassled going into the police station and seeing if they had any more information about Jay Brill.

'How's the art project going, Seb?'
  'Slow, Mum.'
  'What's it about?'
  'Connections.'
  'And what are you supposed to produce?' Seb's dad
reached across the table for the mustard.
  'That's the thing, Dad . . . I can do what I like. Makes it
even harder, you know?'
  'Have you had any ideas?'
It was dinner. Seb wondered if it would follow the normal
question-and-answer format. With him in the hot seat.
  'I've been thinking a lot about the tube map, like you told
me about.'
  'Interesting . . . what're you going to do with it?'
  'Don't know yet, it's just the start of an idea. I've got to
take it on some more, find out where it could go . . . make
loads of sketches and stuff so they can see my thought
processes.'
  'You could always do that bit *after* you've done the finished piece . . . it's called post-rationalisation, everybody
does it, they have the brilliant idea in the first five minutes
and then they've got to work up enough background to
justify the enormous fee they want to charge.'
Seb's dad was the studio manager at a design group,
which, he said, meant he was where the buck stopped. To
say he could be stressed out was putting it mildly.
  'Is that really the kind of attitude you want Seb to have?'
  Silence.
Seb recognised this as one of those moments where war

was likely to break out, with his parents pulling the pins on a whole series of verbal grenades. Normally Seb would find an excuse to make himself scarce, leaving the two of them to fight it out in a series of increasingly bitter skirmishes. But it was going to be hard to get out of the firing line in the middle of a meal.

'I know what I was going to ask you guys . . . '

Both his parents turned to look at him. It was like being the target in a shooting gallery.

'I saw some symbols . . . some graphics, and I don't know what they mean . . . wondered whether either of you might know.'

'Graphics?' his dad asked.

'Yeah, they were written somewhere and I copied them. Thought I might be able to use them, but it would be good to know what they were if I did . . . can I just nip up to my room and get them?'

Neither of them had a clue what the symbols were but, by the time that had been established, the possibility of an argument, like a summer squall, had blown over. Seb could-n't work out why his parents, who seemed to be quite happy with each other – had spent the last 25 or so years together, ferchristsake! – argued so much about such stupid little things. You'd think the reason why people stayed together so long was because they agreed about a lot of stuff, not the exact opposite. As they were always saying on crap American sitcoms: go figure.

The next day he had to go into college. It was the first time back since 'the incident', as his mum had insisted she went in to get books and stuff for him when he'd got well enough to start working again. Well enough to work, not to walk. Mums, dontcha just love 'em?

He'd been at the school since he was, what? 12? Year 7, anyway. And now it was strange how distant from it he felt, like he'd grown up, moved on and outgrown it. And yet there was still an odd sense of belonging. He'd spent an awful lot of his time there, he was safe inside the wire, cocooned from the rest of the world. He was understood there, if not exactly valued very highly.

But that day up west had changed everything. It was like putting on a pair of 3D glasses and suddenly being able to see the world in a different way. Same place, new perspective, new point of view. He had the clearer picture, now all he had to do was try and understand what the hell it meant.

He was making his way to an English revision tutorial when he heard his name being called and he turned to see Steve and Adam, two guys he knew by sight, but had never hung with. They were beckoning him over.

'Heard you nearly karcked it, Sebbo.' Steve made a stupid face.

'Didn't know you were into the serious shit.' Adam stared at him in a reappraising kind of way.

'You kicked it now?' Steve, who'd been hanging back, moved in nearer.

'What're you lot on about? I got beaten up by some homeless maniac.'

'We heard you overdosed on something,' Adam smiled, looking over at Steve.

'Heroin,' Steve nodded.

'You OK now?' Adam flicked hair out of his eyes. 'Was it hard to kick? I heard it was a bastard doing that.'

'Leave it out, guys . . . where'd you hear all this crap anyway?'

'Dunno.' Adam now looked slightly disappointed. 'Someone said you'd been found in the street, you know, an ambulance job?'

'Yeah, some junkie phoned you in after you collapsed,' Steve nodded.

'Jesus,' Seb shook his head. 'It was *nothing* like that . . . does everyone think I'm a *junkie* now?'

'Pretty common knowledge, Sebbo,' Adam shrugged.

'You saying it's all, like, a load of bullshit?'

'I did end up in Intensive Care, but otherwise, yeah, it's all a load of bullshit, Steve.'

'You were, like, bunking off though.' Adam jerked a thumb in a general out-of-school direction.

'True,' Seb smiled. 'The rumour factory got that bit right.'

'OK . . . we'll see you later, Sebbo.' Adam patted his shoulder.

'Later, guys.' Seb watched them walk away and wondered how the hell he'd managed to get this reputation as a whacked-out smackhead.

'Penny for them.'

Seb turned to his right to see Mrs Sanders, his year tutor, standing behind him, head on one side, observing.

'Sorry?'

'You look very pensive, Seb. Everything OK? This is your first day back, isn't it?'

'Yeah . . . '

'How are you?'

'Fine.'

'As well as can be expected?'

'Something like that.'

'They're worse than a bunch of tabloid gossip columnists, those boys.'

'Sorry?'

'I've got a fair idea what they were saying . . . my advice is to just ignore them and they'll go away, eventually.'

'I'm fine.'

'Why let the truth get in the way of a good story, eh?' Mrs Sanders looked in the direction Adam and Steve had gone in.

'Crap way of doing things, going round believing lies . . . it's like if I still believed in Santa or the tooth fairy. Or God.'

'Do you want to talk about what happened?'

'I don't want to *not* talk about it . . . like it never happened. Like at home.'

'My door's always open.'

'Yeah, well, thanks . . . '

'No pressure, Seb, no pressure.'

'OK.' Seb turned to go off to his tutorial and then stopped. 'Mrs Sanders?'

'Yes?'

'Could you look at something for me . . . see if you know what it means?'

'Of course,' she said, sneaking a glance at her watch. 'What is it?'

'D'you know what these are?' He held out the stat of the symbols Jay Brill had tattooed on his forearms.

'Let me see . . . ' Mrs Sanders put on the pair of half-glasses that were her trademark; they were either hanging round her neck on an overly elaborate gold chain or she was peering at you over them.

'No one seems to know anything about them . . . I saw them somewhere and thought they looked interesting.'

'They're Greek.' Mrs Sanders looked up. 'This one, the one like the sideways lapel ribbon, is one way of writing alpha – like our letter a – and this one is zeta, or our zed.'

'Really? An a and a zed?'

'Yes,' Mrs Sanders gave Seb back the stat, 'although in the Greek alphabet zed isn't the last letter . . . that's omega, like the watch company.'

'Yeah?' Seb wondered why Jay Brill would have two Greek letters tattooed on his arms.

'You'd better get to your tutorial, Seb . . . and don't forget what I said about my door being open.'

'OK – and, um, thanks for the info.'

'My pleasure,' Mrs Sanders smiled, 'it's good to have you back . . . I'm glad to see that you're taking the exams seriously.'

'Yeah . . . ' Seb looked down, waiting for the inevitable 'This isn't a rehearsal, you know' lecture he'd already had several times in his school career.

'And lucky you had that guardian angel looking out for you,' said Mrs Sanders. 'You know you must be doing something right when you've got a friend like that.'

How, wondered Seb as he made his way to his tutorial, was it possible for someone to get it so wrong?

CHAPTER 10

JUST WHAT HAD MRS SANDERS MEANT BY HIM having a guardian angel, anyway? Someone to watch over him? But why him? Every time he started thinking about this thing of having been chosen it freaked him. At school, being chosen for something usually meant you were the sucker who had to pick up the shitty end of the stick, do the job no one else wanted to do. Or be the one who had to stand in front of all your friends and make a royal fool of yourself. Either way, being chosen was rarely like winning the lottery and he wasn't used to it having an up side.

Seb was still on the school grounds. Having finished the tutorial, he'd decided that a visit to the art department mightn't be such a bad idea. Show his face, run some ideas past Mr Raymond. Get some steer, as his dad would put it. He could show him the symbols as well, get his take on them.

Now at least he knew what they were, which was at least something. Except that he still didn't know what the reason behind them was – was there a story attached to Jay Brill having those particular symbols tattooed on his arms? But he didn't think finding out was going to be as easy as asking a teacher . . . I mean, why would anyone want to have two random letters inked on their body for ever, anyway?

Maybe, as they weren't Jay Brill's initials, they were those of someone who meant a lot to him. Maybe he had a Greek girlfriend or wife . . . or a Greek mother? Who the hell knew. Face it, they could mean nothing. He stood for a moment in the sun, realising that the truth was he'd gone one step forward only to find he'd taken two steps back in the process. Why did it feel like he was a player in a game where someone kept changing the rules without telling him?

The art department was all the way over the campus in North Wing, and to get there he had to weave his way through wave after wave of Year 8s and 9s as they came milling up the slope towards him, like weary salmon to their spawning grounds. As he reached the first outbuildings of the school's other wing he got that odd feeling, somehow in the middle of his head, that he was being watched. Not watched over. Observed.

He stopped, letting the final stragglers weave past him, and looked around. It took a moment, then he saw her. Shona. She was about 50 metres away, over by the science building, leaning back against the wall, one foot propped up behind her. So calm, so cool and so couldn't give a fuck.

It was the first time he'd seen her since the day before getting trashed by the psycho. They'd had a real screamer of a row, during which Shona had walked out and they hadn't spoken since; the only communication they'd had was the text from her that had helped push him off towards the bus stop rather than college that day. And now there she was, looking like she expected him to walk over and talk to her; apologise, probably.

Not going to happen.

He'd been through so much over the last few weeks, and

he'd basically done it on his own. There'd been more than a few times he could've done with someone close to talk to, she must've known that, but the bitch had never called, never sent a note, nothing. True, he hadn't called her, but right at the start, when he was in hospital, there was no way he could. And by the time he came home, there was no way he would. She'd blown it. Anyway, wasn't she supposed to have a new boyfriend?

He turned his back to her and began walking towards the main North Wing building. Sod the art department for today. Sod the lot of them. If he was going to have to do this by himself he'd fucking do it by himself. As he walked through the building and out into the car park he realised he was angry, just-so-bloody-angry about being abandoned by everyone, and even though a small part of him knew that he was more than partly to blame for becoming the kind of person who could be deserted, these thoughts were drowned out by the rising heat of his outrage. Fuel to the fire that kept him walking away from the college.

'Sebbo!'

Seb glanced to his left and saw Adam and Steve across the street. They were waving for him to come over and join them. And why the hell not.

'Easy . . . what's happening?'

Adam looked at Steve and Steve giggled. Seb caught the whiff of spliff.

'Fancy some?' Steve let Seb see the thin little joint he was cupping in his palm.

'We're going round a mate's place,' said Adam.

'Anyone I know?'

'Prob'ly not.'

'He's got all sorts of stuff . . . all sorts,' Steve grinned.

'Liquorice bloody allsorts!' Adam snorted.

Seb watched the two of them collapse into a fit of giggles, holding each other up, tears in their eyes.

'D'you geddit?'

'Liquori-i-i-ice!' Steve sniggered, immediately going off on one again.

'I get it . . . so where we going, guys?'

'Right, right . . . we're – where are we going, Stevie?'

'Martin's . . . we're going to bloody Martin's.'

Martin. It was like, one way or the other, the man was going to get him, catch him in one of his nets, so why not just get it over and done with? He could handle it now. He really could. But as Seb walked off down the street with Steve and Adam, something stopped him from letting on that he knew all about Martin. Way more, he reckoned, than they did.

He let them take him the long way round to the ground-floor flat Martin used as a base. He lived somewhere up in Barnet, Hadley Wood or something like that, but the flat in the oldish, five-storey block at the end of the High Street was where you always met him. He watched Adam press the button for Flat 4 and, having said who he was, let him lead the way after they'd been buzzed in.

Standing outside the flat Seb could hear the deadbolts being thrown, all four of them, and then the door to the flat was opened, as far as the chain would let it, by a small, pale woman with short, dyed-blonde hair, deep red lipstick and too much mascara. Kelly. No one knew what her exact relationship with Martin was, but wherever he went, there she was. At first glance she looked young, but her eyes, behind the black, underneath the lines, were old. Instead of letting them in she kept the chain on, looking accusingly at Seb as she spoke to Adam.

'Why's he with you?'

'Friend of ours, Kelly.' Adam looked back at Seb.

'He's cool, honest,' Steve's head nodded like a puppet.

'Why're you here again so soon, Adam?' Kelly still hadn't moved.

'Run out, didn't we.'

'You got cash on you?' Kelly rubbed her thumb and fore-finger together, glancing at Seb but still not saying any-thing. Seb figured she wanted to see what Martin would do when he walked into the room.

'Got, you know, a bit.' Adam looked at Steve.

'I've got some.' Seb didn't know what had made him say it, maybe it was just to get them out of the corridor. He felt uneasy standing there, waiting.

'See, I told you he was OK!' Steve grinned, patting Seb on the back.

'All right, come on.' Kelly closed the door, unhooked the chain and let them into the flat.

The place was dark, as usual. Same old blood-red walls and deep pile carpet in the corridor and the room they were taken to, same thick red velvet curtains, drawn against the day. The only light coming from the massive gas plasma TV screen.

'Back again, boys.' Martin was sitting in the black leather recliner. He was dressed, as ever, all in black, wearing tinted glasses and watching cable TV, flicking through the channels at random, nothing on screen for longer than 15 seconds. He looked at Seb but didn't say a word, like he'd never seen him before. 'What can I do for you?'

'That stuff we had last time?' Adam shuffled, awkward, from foot to foot.

'What was that . . . Purple Haze?'

'Yeah,' Steve nodded.

'None left, boys, all sold out and not expecting any more till end of next week . . . I can do you a nice tidy daughter of White Widow for a pony. Blow your fucking heads off, that will.'

Adam looked over at Steve, frowning slightly, and Seb saw Steve shrug. Looked like neither of them knew what the hell Martin was on about, but he wasn't going to say anything.

'What about it then . . . quarter of an ounce for a straight fifty quid, can't say fairer than that.'

'Seb?' Adam glanced at him, eyebrows raised.

'I got £20.'

'OK . . . could we, like, get a wotsit . . . half that?'

'A Henry? I can do that – Kelly, wrap up an eighth of the Widow for the boys!' He held out the hand that wasn't clicking the remote. 'Gimme 25, and until you start getting serious about doing some proper business for me, you can stop coming round. This isn't a fucking 7/11.'

'OK . . . right.' Adam's smile was the most desperate thing Seb had ever seen.

'Is that a yes or a no?'

'It's a . . . ' Adam looked frantically at Steve, who nodded. 'It's a yes, Martin.'

'What about the new boy, he in too?'

'Sure, sure, he's cool.' Steve grinned manically at Seb and Adam, nodding even more like a Thunderbird puppet.

Seb watched Martin. He was playing with Adam and Steve, but they were too stupid to know it. He was messing with him as well, pretending they'd never met, so, Seb reckoned, whatever Martin wanted to say to him, he was going to have to wait to find out. He handed some notes over to Adam, who wouldn't look at him straight in the eye.

'Come and see me next week, say Wednesday . . . bring your friend, he looks like he knows what's what.' Martin fired the remote like an Uzi at the TV, channels switching every couple of seconds, as he took the money. 'Now bugger off, and if I hear you've been bragging, I'll not be pleased.'

They walked back out into the reality of the High Street with their deal: an eighth of an ounce of primo skunk. It meant they even had enough money left in the kitty for a six-pack of Diamond White, some cans of Carlsberg and a handful of Mars bars and stuff. Sorted, grinned Steve. But Adam seemed less than pleased.

'What's he want us to bring *you* back for, eh Seb?'

'Don't ask me.'

'But I *am* asking Sebbo.' Adam poked Seb in the ribs, too hard to be friendly, not hard enough to provoke a physical response. Which was when Seb's phone went.

'Yeah?' Seb could see it was Martin calling.

'You're back . . . why didn't you call? I thought you said you'd call when you were better.'

'*You* said it, not me.'

'Whatever . . . ' Seb could hear the TV channels changing every few seconds in the background. 'What are you doing with that pair of dim bulbs anyway?'

'Nothing much . . . ' Seb watched Adam watch him as he talked, trying to listen without looking like he was.

'Have fun doing it . . . I'll see you later.'

'Right . . . ' Shutting the phone, Seb felt like he'd warped back to before going AWOL and ending up in hospital. Like nothing had changed. Like nothing ever would.

'Who was that then?' Adam smiled, no humour in it. 'Shona, was it?'

'None of your business, Adam, OK?'

'Look . . . '

'What is it with you two?' Steve butted in. 'Where are we off to anyway?'

Fifteen minutes later they were at the back end of what was laughingly called a nature reserve by the local council. It was a couple of acres of scrub that had been left to get on with it, the kind of place that was a bit iffy even in broad daylight, let alone after dark. The perfect place to get ripped, undisturbed by just about any form of authority. Which is what they proceeded to do.

They started with the cider and the lager, Adam rolling them a very large spliff each; lighting up they began working on the chocolate bars. Adam and Steve were already partly loaded, but Seb soon caught them up as he hadn't smoked for weeks, hadn't eaten since breakfast and the skunk was wickedly powerful.

'Jesus, this is strong . . . '

'Martin dun't do rubbish, Sebbo.' Steve took a big hit and fell backwards on to the grass, giggling again.

'So you guys gonna be, like, working for him?' Seb drew and held.

'Might be . . . ' Adam looked sideways at Seb, eyes slitted. 'But like he said, we're not s'posed to say anything, right?'

'Safe.'

'Why're you so interested anyway, man?'

'No big deal . . . I was just kind of curious, you know.' Seb lit his joint again. 'That Martin's not pissing around, is he . . . I mean, it's a proper set-up he's got there, nothing like Jon the Hat.'

'The Hat's nowhere, man,' Steve mumbled. 'Martin does *everything*, man . . . he can get . . . '

'Fucking shut it, Steve!' Adam kicked him, hard, glancing back at Seb. 'And just stop asking questions, right? No questions.'

'That bloody hurt, man . . . ' Steve sat up, massaging his leg .

'Serves you right.'

'Stop being so fucking paranoid, ferchristsake, will you?' Steve moved out of Adam's range. 'What is it with you anyway?'

'Nothing's with me.' Adam's eyes shifted quickly between Seb and Steve as he sat, tensed, nervously picking at a hangnail on his thumb.

A cloud went across the sun, casting them in shadow and making Seb shiver involuntarily. The whole mood had changed, there was a nasty edge now, on top of which he was starting to feel like shit. He put his bottle down and it fell over, spilling cider on to the grass. He left it there, hugging himself as he felt his stomach roll.

'You all right?' Steve peered at Seb. 'Look, Ad, he looks fucking dreadful.'

'He's just got the whites,' Adam got up, 'he'll be OK.'

'Where you going, Ad?'

'Home.'

'Wait for me.' Steve got up. 'Give us a hand with Sebbo.'

'Piss off, Steve . . . let him sort himself out . . . '

Seb watched Adam stumble off. Watched Steve follow him out of sight, whining about how he hadn't done anything. And then he was all on his own. Cold and sweaty, shivering and feeling like he might chuck at any moment. There was no point in calling for help, they'd come here because there'd be no one else around, and he was a good twenty minutes' walk from home. A good twenty minutes if he was feeling OK, and not like he was about to pass out.

He slumped sideways and curled into a ball, groaning. Why he'd gone to Martin's with Adam and Steve he couldn't really say. Lying on the grass, the tiny bit of his brain that wasn't dealing with imminent meltdown could only think it was probably being hacked off with Shona that had made him act like a twat. Like a part of his head had glommed on to what Mrs Sanders had said and might believe he really did have a guardian angel. Crap logic dictating that *if* he did, nothing bad would happen to him, no matter what he got up to.

Only a fool would try and test out a rubbish theory like that . . .

CHAPTER 11

KNEELING ON THE GROUND, STILL FEELING LIKE he was going to be sick at any moment, Seb knew he'd be in real trouble if his mum found out what he'd been up to; he'd have to be extra careful getting himself back into the house, cos if she saw him looking like shit, she'd be down on him like a ton of bricks. In her mind there was no way he wasn't still an invalid. He felt lucky she didn't mash his food up.

And so much for having a guardian angel. But then what the hell would Jay Brill be doing wandering round some scuzzy north London nature reserve anyway? What had got into his head that he thought he could get away with anything he wanted?

After what seemed like ages Seb finally started to feel slightly better, got himself up and made his way out of the scrub. He still felt rancid, and thought, from the glances he had from a couple of people as he walked home, that he must look pretty shabby as well. How different from the way it'd been this morning as he left home to go to college.

It was coming up to four o'clock by the time he got to his street. This was where it got tricky. His mum worked at a local primary school, assistant to the head teacher. She worked four days a week and got home at five . . . the question was, was this one of the days she worked, or was it a day off? Seb wished he paid more attention to what was going on in his house.

Outside the house there was no car on what had once been a front garden, but was now a decorative brick parking area. That meant nothing, because he had no idea which of his parents had taken the car that morning. Did he phone on his mobile and see if his mum picked up, then hang up? Or should he just ever-so-quietly try the door, see if it was double locked? If it was he was home free.

Hanging about on the pavement made him feel nervous and he decided to take the lock route. He listened at the door for a moment, straining to see if he could hear a radio or something, then tried the Yale. The door didn't open. Seb realised he'd been holding his breath, let it out with a whistle and fumbled the second key into the lock.

'Hello, thought you'd've been back ages ago.'

'Mum!' Seb whirled round, like he'd been caught red-handed breaking in; his mum was standing right behind him. Holding a couple of bulging Asda bags.

'You look as if you've seen a ghost . . . are you OK? You've not done too much today, have you?'

'I'm fine, Mum.' Seb slapped a last-minute smile on his face and tried to look like he meant it. 'Honest.'

'How was the tutorial? Was it tiring being back?'

'No, no, it was OK . . . fine.'

'Did you see Mr Whatsisname, your art tutor?'

'Mr Raymond, no . . . he wasn't there.' Seb turned back to open the front door, smile still frozen on his face. 'I, um, I did see Mrs Sanders, my, you know, year tutor? I showed her those symbols? She told me they were the Greek letters for an a and a zed.'

'Ancient Greek?'

'Just Greek, far as I know.' Seb stood back, looking at his feet as he let his mum into the house.

'I'm gasping for a cuppa . . . d'you fancy one?'

'You couldn't do me an egg 'n' bacon sandwich as well, could you?' Nothing like pushing your luck. 'I'm going upstairs to do some work on my art project.'

'I'll give you a call when it's ready.'

Seb sat at his desk, feeling like one lucky bastard. Talk about acting guilty, he must've had a bloody great big flashing arrow pointing at him. How he'd got away with that he didn't know. Then again, a lot of his panic could've been down to the draw . . . a bad case of dope paranoia. Come to think of it, the only person who *hadn't* seemed to have been affected by the White Widow was Steve – possibly too thick to know what paranoia was. Seb realised Adam must've got it bad, though, cos he'd really been giving him the evil eye – probably not a happy bunny about him and Martin. Which was fine, because neither was Seb.

To get Martin out of his head, Seb scanned the mess of papers in front of him and eventually found what he was looking for: the art project brief. He was supposed to have been working on it for at least a term, as part of his course, but, like everything else to do with his A Levels, he'd left it till the last minute. And this was just about as last minute as you could get.

The previous two years had just been so full on dull. He couldn't remember being so bored, never felt less like doing stuff and more like everything he was supposed to do was pointless. He scanned the stapled sheets in front of him. Right at the top the heading said, 'Connections', and the gist of the brief was that he should fully investigate the concept of connections, blah, blah, blah, and produce something – his choice of medium – that made some kind of original comment about it.

He was about to get pissed off, chuck the brief back on the desk and find something else to do, when he heard an echo of Billy Swift, sitting at the caff table, telling him not to regret what he'd done, but what he didn't do. Much as he'd had it with his English and his art, he was now so near getting it all over and done with that it would be rank stupidity not to try and get the best result he could. Wouldn't it? God, he was beginning to sound like his own parents.

He looked at the brief again. He could do this. He really could.

Seb's mind immediately went blank, as if every idea he was ever likely to have had fled the moment it'd heard it might be needed. He picked up a pad and a pencil and waited. Something was bound to happen. It had to.

He was rescued from having to sit around waiting to find out by the sound of his mother calling him from downstairs. Maybe he'd be better equipped for being creative with some food inside him.

'D'you want ketchup, Seb?'

'Ummmm . . . '

'Mustard's in the fridge if you'd prefer that.'

'Thanks.' Seb put his mug down and got up from the kitchen table to take the toasted sandwich and ketchup bottle his mum was holding out. 'Ketchup's fine, Mum.'

'How's the project going? Is this the one you were talking about, that you'd been thinking of doing something on the tube map?'

He stopped, egg and bacon toastie poised and ready to

97

accept a squirt of tomato sauce, and looked open-mouthed at his mum.

'Joy oh-joy oh-joy!'

'What did I say?'

'My brain must be on hold, it really must.' Seb shook his head. 'I've just wasted God knows how long trying to think of something, and I've already thought of it!'

'Glad to be of assistance . . . '

Tube map. Fine. Now what? It wasn't as if he was the first person to have ever tried to think of a way to use something in a whole *other* way and call it art. Like that bloke who'd signed a men's bog, called it 'Fountain' and entered it into an exhibition. Mr Raymond said it was art because the guy had chosen it. Well, maybe. It was sort of like Andy Warhol hijacking products or famous people's faces and just repeating them. How easy was that? No wonder so many people did conceptual art nowadays. Except it only really worked if you were the originator, the first person to think of doing it, and the rest was just blagging.

It seemed like everything eventually got used by artists wanting a short cut, wanting to do it the easy way. Which meant that if Seb were going to do something that wasn't just blagging, he had to take the tube map idea on further. Then it occurred to him – what if he made his own map . . . made his own connections? He picked up his pencil again and began scribbling.

Underground. Maps. Roads. Crossroads. Intersections. Contours. Colours. Height. Depth. Perspective. Point of view. Vista. Landscape. Heart. Soul. Feeling. Nerves. Spine. Veins. Arteries. Web. Network. Edge. Perimeter. Flow. Ebb. 3D. Relief. Elevation. Angles. Projection. Plan.

As he wrote with one hand, he flicked through a succession of design and art books on his lap with the other, looking at pictures, reading captions, turning back to catch something that had flashed past him too quickly. At some point in the process, from some dusty corner of his mental filing system, the image of Pinhead from the Clive Barker movie *Hellraiser* slid into his head for no specific reason he could fathom. They had the video downstairs, one of his dad's extensive collection of what he called screamers. The aptly named Pinhead was on the cover. Seb sat back.

Nails.

He wrote the word down. You could make a contour map using nails of different lengths . . . viewed from straight in front it should get a certain texture from the size of the nail heads, like the dots in a black and white photo in the newspaper. Viewed from an angle – *lit* from a different angle, now there was an idea! And if you changed the light source – light sources? – the shadows would make the piece look like it was moving. Nice.

He was idly flicking through pages, about to close the book he was holding, when an image grabbed his attention and he turned back to find it again. It was a drawing. A beautiful, clear artwork of something that looked like a time-elapse figure of a man; he was shown in two overlapping poses, framed by a circle on a square. Drawn by . . . he searched for the information . . . Leonardo da Vinci. He'd done it, said the text, to show perfect human proportion, but as Seb was drawn further into the picture, staring at the soulful face, he got something different from it. Other information.

He felt the man looked, on the one hand, trapped by the square, but at the same time was somehow trying to break free in the circle. In the square he was almost *robotic*, with lines on his joints that seemed to bind him, to keep him in place. In the circle he flew. He was someone who existed in two different, linked places. Connected.

Seb felt that way himself sometimes. He existed at home, as the person his parents thought he was, trapped in the box that was their idea of him, and then there was his world outside. The person he was becoming.

OK.

Seb stayed very still. Almost like, if he moved, the idea would break, or disappear, never to come back, as dreams often did when you started them too near the surface and were woken up. He looked at the picture of the Leonardo drawing and tried to imagine what his next step was. Where did he go from here? His eyes flicked over to the pad he'd been scribbling on and he wrote down *Leonardo man* and underlined it. Then he underlined *Nails* and *Underground* as well.

Still OK.

He looked at the drawing again, a feeling nagging at him from the back of his head that it was like something he'd seen somewhere before, but he couldn't think what it was. And then it dawned on him. The Angel of the North. Bloody wonderful sculpture, a massive thing, high up on a hill outside Newcastle. He'd seen it last year when they'd driven up to Scotland to visit relatives, had thought about asking his dad to take a detour up to see it on the way back, but hadn't bothered in the end. And afterwards wished he had (thank you, Billy Swift).

Seb wrote down *Angel* and underlined it. Twice.

He realised he felt excited. Not the scared, itchy excitement that you got from doing stuff you maybe shouldn't, the excitement he kind of recognised as being fuelled by a swift hit of adrenalin. This was different. He felt as if there was a hidden side to his intelligence, like a separate part of himself he hadn't encountered before, which was playing with him, teasing and tempting him. Was some part of his subconscious feeding thoughts and ideas to his conscious mind . . . and, if it was, which bit of him controlled the creativity? Or was it the two sides of himself working together that made him feel that, right now, nothing was impossible . . .

Leonardo man. *Nails*. *Underground*. *Angel*.

Seb drew out a simple, 3x4" sketch of the Leonardo drawing with a soft pencil on a new page of his pad. He picked up a fine-nib black felt-tip and started creating a dot version of the image. Then he reached for a flat, oblong tin of coloured pencils, opened it and picked out one of the red ones; starting at the top he joined up a set of random dots and then swapped colours.

When he'd finished he tore the page out and pinned it up next to Billy's picture of Jay Brill and the Greek symbols. His fingers tingled. He felt exhausted and elated at the same time, like when you surprise yourself by winning a race you thought you had no chance in.

Up there on the wall was a real live idea, waiting for him to take it off the page and make it happen. Make it big. Would he be able to do it? Could it all crumble and turn to dust? Only one way to find out. Like the shoe man said, just do it.

What a truly bizarre day . . .

CHAPTER 12

LATER, AFTER SUPPER, SEB WENT OUT INTO THE back garden for a fag. It was a warm night with a clear sky that he knew, in a less well-lit place, would be lavishly dusted with millions and millions of stars. But London – any big smoke, probably – had a kind of radioactive glow that meant the night was never truly dark. He sat, his feet up on a garden chair, and watched the pale, fluid line from his cigarette curl upwards almost straight, weaving snake-like, curiously oily patterns in the still air, then fading to nothing.

'Mind if I join you?'

Seb looked round to see his dad, silhouetted against the kitchen window. 'Sure,' he said, shifting his feet off the chair and pushing it towards his father. Something must be up. His dad never hung out for chats, and that's what he sounded like he wanted.

'Beer?'

Beer? Seb looked at the bottle of Bud he was being offered.

'It's cold.'

'Thanks . . . '

'We don't talk much, do we.'

'No . . . '

'Your brother always pretty much kept himself to himself . . .

it sort of becomes a habit you get into, not talking about things. Not talking about anything, really, trivial or important. You end up, well, not knowing who people are. I mean, you know what me and your mum do, but I bet you know as little about what we think as we do about what's going on inside your head.'

Seb took a pull of beer. Had Mrs Sanders been having a word? He'd only been saying to her that day about how nothing was ever said in his house. And now it was and he didn't know how to react.

'Cat got your tongue?'

'What? No . . . I mean, yeah, you're right.'

'Your bedroom light was on . . . I saw that stuff on your pinboard when I was turning it off . . . the symbols and the kind of Leonardo thing.'

'You know about that?'

'I didn't always run a graphics studio, Seb . . . back in the mists of time I was an art student, did art A level, just like you. Who was the portrait of, by the way?'

'Oh . . . that, um, it's just some bloke . . . a friend of mine did it.'

'It's very good – someone from college?'

'No . . . no, a guy I met doing my, you know, research.' Seb fidgeted himself into a more comfortable position. 'What did you think of the idea?'

'Idea?'

'The Leonardo thing, it's my art project . . . the one I was, like, telling you about the other night?'

'I thought I saw a passing reference to the tube map.' His dad took a sip from his bottle. 'It looks interesting. You going to paint it?'

'Thinking of doing something with nails and stuff.' Seb

leant forward. 'I thought I could also use lights to make shadows?'

'Full size?'

'How d'you mean?'

'Is it going to be based on you?'

Which was how Seb found himself, the next morning, spread-eagled on a two-metre square piece of 25mm-thick MDF, while his dad checked what they were doing against the picture in the art book. The bloke at the woodyard who was serving them was looking at them like they were totally barking.

He and his dad had stayed in the garden till way after midnight, planning the construction of the Leonardo project. They'd moved inside when it got too cold and ended up covering the kitchen table with roughs and lists of materials and coloured sketches.

When they'd eventually packed it in, Seb went to bed wondering why they'd never done stuff like that before. It wasn't as if his dad had been an absentee father or anything, he'd been around but they didn't ever seem to *do* anything together. Not that he remembered asking, or ever feeling he was missing out on anything because his dad didn't take him fishing or off to football matches or whatever.

They still hadn't talked about 'the incident', but he had to be honest, it hadn't even occurred to him to mention it, he'd been so engrossed in the planning they'd been doing. Better to be talking about something than nothing at all, he thought as he turned his bedside light off.

The MDF was now in his bedroom. Just. It had taken bloody for ever to get it up the stairs and through the door and it was now propped up against his bookcase, dominating the room. At least he knew what he was going to do with it, because having a blank canvas that size, and no ideas, would be enough to put anyone off for life.

On the floor in front of the MDF was a tin of white under-coat, a massive can of white gloss spray paint, a couple of brushes, a folded plastic dustsheet, a hammer and about a dozen boxes of various sizes of nails. An art kit. All he had to do now was start. Actually, all he had to do now was go back up to the DIY shop and get the small can of black gloss paint he'd forgotten.

Seb kind of sensed he was being followed almost as soon as he started walking up to the High Street. For a truly frightening couple of minutes, his bastard imagination insisted that it was Zack coming up behind him and he couldn't physically turn round. Then he got a grip and glanced over his shoulder. Adam and Steve. Steve waved when he saw Seb had clocked them, Adam looking at Steve like he was a bad smell. Seb stopped walking.

'You going my way?'

'Wanted a word, Sebbo mate.' Adam stood about a metre and a half away, Steve shuffling behind him, sniffing. 'Tha's all.'

'No problem . . . what about?'

'Martin says to say he kind of wants to see you . . . you know, now.'

'And?'

'What? Yeah . . . like, he wants you to come up to the flat with us.'

'No.'

'See, I told you, Ad.'

'Shut it, Stevie – why not?'

'Why not? Cos I've got enough on my plate with the As coming up and I don't need any of what Martin's up to right now.'

'Who gives a flying fuck about the exams, Sebbo . . . what are you suddenly, some kind of swot? This'll give you serious cash right now. Instant, mate, just like the lottery.'

'No lie, man . . . Martin's dead straight for a, you know, dealer . . . '

'Fuck it, Stevie – how many times you have to be told?'

'I know what Martin does, Adam.'

'How come, Sebbo . . . how come you know so much?'

Seb ignored Adam's question, looking away as he spoke. 'Can't go, got stuff on . . . I'm in the middle of something.'

'What's with you, Sebbo, man?' Adam moved in closer.

'Nothing.'

'You gotta come, we promised we'd bring you back with us.'

'Go and *un*promise.'

Seb turned and began to walk away.

'You *fucker*!'

The next thing Seb knew, Adam had leapt on him and grabbed his jacket, pulling him backwards. He spun round, breaking Adam's grip, and faced him up, now only inches away. Adam had pinholes for pupils.

'Leave it out, Adam . . . whatever you're on, just leave it out.' Seb backed off slightly, throwing a glance at Steve, but he was skulking, nervously flicking a Cricket lighter and looking like he wished he were anywhere else but there. Seb knew exactly how he felt; the last thing he needed right now was a fight. 'Go and tell Martin you made a mistake, tell him I found God, left the country, tell him anything you like, but include me out of any more of your plans. OK?'

'You fucking *nonce*!'

'Whatever.' Seb hadn't moved, but there was now a couple of feet between the two of them.

'You can't walk out on this . . . ' Now Adam was beginning to sound like Steve. 'Martin said . . . '

'Screw what Martin said – you shouldn't believe everything you're told, man . . . ' Seb didn't need this, he *really* didn't need it. He leant forward. 'Leave-me-alone, OK?'

Adam flinched. 'Don't stress, man . . . '

Seb stabbed a finger at him, but he couldn't think of anything to say that wouldn't sound totally crap, so he just walked off up the road. Behind him he heard Steve's monotone whine and Adam telling him to fuck off. Dullards. You had to wonder what Martin was up to, having anything at all to do with the Dim Twins . . .

Even with all the windows wide open, the room reeked of acetone and Seb still had the memory of a thunderous headache, thumping like a muffled bass drum, at the back of his head. Tonight he was sleeping in his brother's room. And he could swear he'd hammered thousands of nails into the MDF, once the paint had dried. Millions. His fingers were numb and he was still nowhere near finished. Leaning against the opposite wall, hammer hanging from one hand, unlit fag from the other, it occurred to him that he hadn't figured out how he was going to do the colour on the piece, make the actual connections.

He and his dad had got as far as how to undercoat and gloss the MDF, then mask the whole thing with newspaper, do the nails and finally spray the nails black. But that was all they'd got figured. Seb was about to light his cigarette, but instead pushed himself off the wall and went out for some fresh air. He'd likely blow the whole place up smoking in his bedroom.

It was late, but his parents were out somewhere. The pub, a meal with friends, he couldn't remember what they'd told him. In the kitchen he made himself a cup of coffee, raided the biscuit jar and switched on the little TV, idly flicking through the channels – 1, 2, 3, 4, TV not tuned for 5, so back to 1, 2, 3 and the ad break must be over because there was a movie on now. Some late-night thing, American, an old lady sitting in a rocking chair, telling some bloke called Willard – her grandson? – what a goldarn fool he was even to *think* of going back into town for that no-good hussy of a girl. And as she rocks, back and forth, back and forth, she's sewing coloured thread on to a piece of tapestry that's been clamped into a circular frame.

Eu-bloody-reka!

Seb made straight for the front room and his mum's sewing box. Behind him on the TV he could hear Willard start his car and lay some rubber down as he ignored his gran's advice and went back to town anyway. Seb opened the lid of the box, lifted out the top tray and found himself looking at a rainbow collection of silk thread. There were bright, vibrant reds and greens, shades of blue, from the palest water to electric aquamarine, and any number of yellows, oranges, purples and ultraviolets.

He took the tray out and closed the lid. He was sure his mum wouldn't mind. He'd replace whatever he used. She'd be fine. As he went back upstairs he was already trying to imagine what the threads would look like on the piece. He only had a few thousand more nails to whack in, then spray black, before he'd find out.

CHAPTER 13

ORNING . . . WELL, 11.30. SEB'D WORKED ON the piece until some time around four and then dragged himself off to bed. His parents had come back at about midnight, made encouraging noises and left him to it. Now, his room flooded with midday sunshine, Seb stood and looked at what he'd done.

The massive white square gleamed, its gloss surface almost throwing the sunlight back at him. And standing out, stark against the white background, were all the hundreds of shiny black nails that made up his life-size version of Leonardo's drawing. Running down from the top of the circle to the bottom of the square, like a drop of blood that outlined, head to foot, one side of the body, was a single bright red thread. The last thing he'd done before going to bed.

Was the sodding thing any good? How the hell did he know? But he had to admit it looked OK so far, worth going on with. Which was lucky, cos he already had his work cut out trying to get this idea finished in time as it was.

He'd been so wrapped up in the art project he realised he hadn't thought about Jay Brill or guardian angels for ages. He looked over at the pinboard. Jay Brill's eyes looked back, kind of questioningly, and he found himself feeling guilty, almost like he'd abandoned the man the moment he was better and something more interesting came along. Which was crazy, but Seb still had to turn away.

What was he supposed to do anyway? He had a fixed amount of time and a ton of stuff to get done – and not just the art project. Seb felt himself begin to panic. He always lost the ability to focus on anything when he panicked. It was like a safety mechanism . . . if he couldn't see it clearly, it wasn't there, it didn't matter. This worked for a bit, but things always caught up with him in the end. He could hear his dad, like he was there in the room with him, saying 'What you need is a bit of time management!', which was his standard response when he saw Seb getting screwed by his workload.

OK. Time management. He'd do it. But that meant he would need a diary. Which meant a quick trip to the shops, which worked because walking time was thinking time. All good so far. Go and get the diary, and figure stuff that needed figuring on the way there and back. Weren't plans great?

Because, once you had one, you weren't doing nothing any more, you were in the middle of achieving something. Even if it wasn't very much.

But the trouble with plans was that things didn't always go according to them. Seb had got sidetracked on his way back home. Taking a short cut, the stained-glass windows at the front of an imposing Victorian church had caught his eye. It was a looming gothic pile, all sombre grey stone and happy-clappy notices, a place he'd been past so many times, but he realised he'd never really looked at it properly before.

The two side panels of the triple-arched window were

huge representations of angels. Men, heads surrounded by dinner plates of light, dressed in massive bedsheets, with wings. His 'guardian angel' hadn't looked like that, because if he had people would surely have remembered a lot more about him.

Seb noticed that the door of the church was slightly ajar. The sun was still shining and it occurred to him that to get the full effect of the images he should be doing his viewing from inside the building.

He couldn't remember the last time he'd been into a church. Some aged relative's funeral, or possibly a distant cousin's wedding. One or the other. As he pushed the door open, he seemed to recall a nightmare experience, when he was much younger, involving stiff collars, velvet suits and uncomfortable, very shiny black shoes. Must've been a wedding, then. His footsteps echoed on the old stone flagging as he walked down the main aisle before turning to look up at the window. It was weird how quiet, how peaceful the place was, its thick walls absorbing the noise of the outside world, soaking it up and reducing everything to a low mutter.

Seb stared at the window, now filled with light, the lead strips holding the bits of glass together ink-black against the brilliant, glowing colours. He was amazed by how much painting was involved in a stained-glass window, hadn't really given any thought to how they were made; the complex folds of the cloth were drawn in incredible detail, each feather on every wing was there, individually, and the two angels stood on puffy, marshmallow clouds, either side of a larger figure in the central window. JC. There was something unnaturally calm about their faces, a slightly blissed look. But then they were from heaven.

'Can I help you?'

Seb was jerked back to reality by the sound of the voice. He turned, expecting to find someone standing right behind him, but was surprised to find the person speaking was some way back down the aisle. Acoustics.

'The door was open . . . I just came in to look at the window.'

The man was walking towards him. Nondescript, greying, balding, glasses, dog-collar, wearing a dull burgundy V-neck and grey trousers. A tall, slightly nervous man who looked like the sort of person who was always just about to ask a question.

'I like people to feel they can come in whenever, you know, whenever they want to. Nowadays, though, someone has to be here if the door is unlocked. Which is, um, a shame, but, ah, there you are. You like our window, then?'

'Yeah, it's nice.'

'In the style of Burne-Jones . . . unfortunately not actually *by* Burne-Jones. Wonderful artist . . . he said that he thought a picture was a romantic dream of something that never was and never would be, seen in the best light that ever shone – something like that – and looking at that window always reminds me of the best light that ever shone.'

'D'you, like, believe in angels?'

'Angels?' The vicar looked at Seb, puzzled, as if he'd never considered the subject before, then glanced back at the window. 'I've never seen one, but, yes, I believe in them . . . as part of my faith.'

'So you think they exist?'

'If you believe in something, you have to believe it exists.'

'Even if you've never seen him, I mean it . . . one of them?'

'That's a pretty good definition of faith, don't you think?' the vicar looked over his glasses at Seb, 'Believing in something you don't have proof of?'

What was supposed to have been a short break, with a bit of thinking thrown in, had turned into a marathon angel-quest. After leaving the church, with more questions than answers, Seb couldn't stop brooding about angels. Ever since Mrs Sanders had planted the seed by calling Jay Brill his 'guardian angel', the whole angel thing had been there in the back of his mind, all the time. He couldn't get rid of it. What the fuck was an angel, anyway? There'd been nothing more he could get from the vicar, who had – what was the phrase? – blind faith. Which he kind of needed in his job. And this sort of thing wasn't something he could usefully ask his parents about. They didn't do religion.

That left the Net. All-seeing, all-knowing. Like God on Earth. 'Seek-and-you-will-find' time. Another of his dad's handy little phrases, this one normally used when he directed you towards the dictionary or encyclopedia to look up for yourself whatever it was you wanted to know about.

Back in his room, Jay Brill's picture staring at him from one wall, Leonardo man, like a partially formed ghost, hovering in midair behind him, Seb fired up his computer, switched on the modem and watched the loading screen. Why was it, whenever you were waiting for something, even something fast, it always seemed to be so goddam slow?

Finally he was connected to the Web. But where to go? Alta Vista? Jeeves? Lycos? Google? Excite? So much choice, so many search engines. Because he'd liked the ads on TV, ages ago Seb had made Lycos his default, so he started there, typing in 'Angels', clicking on 'Search'. Within seconds he had the result. Nearly 250,000 sites. A quarter of a bloody million. Before he started looking at any of them he decided to see what a couple of the other engines could do.

Alta Vista. Not too shabby, making Lycos eat dust with a total of just over 2.5 million.

But look at this . . . Google. A clear winner with a staggering 6.68 *million* sites, found in only 0.29 seconds! Hot stuff. He scanned down a couple of screens' worth of sites, soon realising that a lot of them were nothing to do with heavenly angels. Like the Anaheim Angels, which turned out to be a Californian baseball team backed by Disney. Or the Guardian Angels, a group of keep-the-streets-safe vigilante types from the States. And then there were the *Charlie's Angels* TV programme websites and all the ones selling angel stuff. Lots and lots of angel stuff. Paintings, tapestries, museums, figurines, experiences, tattoos. Buy it all at the Angel Mall.

A lot of the sites he visited were the real thing, though. Well, real in that they took the subject of angels totally seriously. Deep, scholarly discussions about the nine different levels of angels – Seraphim, the top dogs, Cherubim, Thrones, Dominions, Virtues, Powers, Principalities, Archangels and finally, bottom of the heap, Angels – as well as hyped-up, tabloid-style articles about 'true' angel stories. A lot of people out there believed in angels, and a lot of *other* people were making wads of money out of them. Belief, like the vicar had said, was everything.

One site he visited, a Catholic one, was typical. It asked questions like, 'How do we know angels exist?', and then didn't answer them, in fact wrote screeds of blah that did everything *but* answer the question. The kind of stuff that'd get you crap marks and sarcastic comments for if you handed it in as an essay.

The same site also said that everyone had their own, personal guardian angel 'to watch over each of us during our lives'. It said that angels were bodiless spirits who could, if they needed to in order to complete their mission, take on human form. Useful.

Where did all this stuff come from? Who made up beliefs anyway? And why was the belief in the nine levels of bodiless spirits any different from believing in myths, legends and fairies? Except everyone over the age of ten knew the truth about fairy tales, so how come so many people never, ever figured out that angels were just as made up, too? Weren't they?

Seb had had it. He logged off the server and shut down. He felt his head was about ready to explode if he carried on arsing about with angels when all he actually had to do was find Jay Brill, shake him by the hand and say his thank yous, like the good boy he was. That would solve everything, because it would turn out Jay was just some bloke who'd been in the right place and done the right thing. And not a bodiless spirit in human form. He'd go back up west tomorrow, have another go at tracking him down, but in the meantime he had a bloody great big piece of art to finish. Seb swung round in his chair to look at it, then down at the silk thread, carefully laid out, red through to violet, on the floor.

He realised that he felt excited about what it could look like when he'd finished it. He had a picture in his head and he really wanted to see if it was going to match what he ended up producing. Seb stretched and stood. No time like the present.

CHAPTER 14

NEXT DAY, AFTER ANOTHER LATE NIGHT, FOLLOWED by an even later morning start, as he'd slept through his alarm, Seb was back on the bus, crawling towards the West End. He liked the bus. It might be slower than the tube, it might stop all the time and you never really knew how long your journey would be, but, up on the top deck, right at the front, you got a bargain basement 'King-of-the-world!' experience. Kind of.

He felt OK about taking some time off from Leonardo man because it was actually looking like it meant something. Coloured threads now criss-crossed the piece, wove intricate patterns in some places and made stark grids in others. In the middle stood the man, trapped yet free. It was, he had to admit, a cool thing to look at. Still a way to go, but unless something went really badly AWOL, the end was in sight. Life was good. And then his mobile went.

'Yeah?'

'Seb.' It wasn't a question.

'Who's that?' He quickly checked the screen: Martin. 'Yeah?'

'I think we need to talk.'

'Why?' Then Seb heard the unmistakable sound of TV channels changing with monotonous regularity in the background. Did the man ever do anything else, like maybe watch a complete programme all the way through?

'I feel let down, sunshine. I had high hopes, if you'll pardon the pun.'

'I don't know what they told you, but I told them thanks, but no thanks. I'm in the middle of my exams, man.'

'Very laudable. But a deal's a deal.'

Deal? 'But I didn't do any deals. No way, specially with Adam and Steve.'

'I don't care.'

Seb waited for more, but all he could hear was static hiss and someone breathing. Was he being threatened? It was hard to tell.

'Forget about Adam and Steve, they're a pair of monkeys . . . I want you back on the team, Sebastian. I've got plans.'

It was Seb's turn to fall silent. Staring out of the bus window, he couldn't think of anything to say. He didn't give a fuck about Martin and his sodding plans, which had nothing to do with him; it was like he was being dragged back into a parallel universe where everything was on repeat.

'I said, I've got plans.'

'Sorry . . . ' Seb didn't know what else to say. He ended the call. Looking at his phone, he wondered what Adam and Steve had told Martin. He cursed himself for the idiot he was for ever having anything to do with the two of them . . . just being seen with them turned him into a plonker by association, and now Martin was rampantly on at him again.

His phone started to ring again. Martin. He switched it off. He knew the man wasn't going to go away that easily, but he didn't want to deal with him now. More important things to do.

Jay Brill could be anywhere but, because he'd been hanging round a soup van late at night, it wasn't likely Seb would find him in Mayfair or Knightsbridge or Kensington. Soho, Covent Garden, King's Cross, Camden, that's where he'd probably be. You had to hope.

He still hadn't been to the cops to ask if they knew anything about the man. It was foolish not to, he knew that, and he could've already saved himself a lot of time and pavement pounding if only he'd got over his almost pathological distrust of them. This was, after all, him going to them, not them hassling him. Getting off the bus at Holborn, intending to do a wide sweep that would take him through to Soho and Piccadilly, he saw a policeman on his beat. If you believed in such things, it was a definite sign.

Seb had been told, he couldn't remember who by, that the police station that had dealt with the assault was Charing Cross. He caught up the policeman some way down from the tube and asked where the station was. Agar Street, off the Strand, the constable said. Not far, if he cut through Covent Garden. Which is how he found himself, about to cross Drury Lane, staring at Crazy Janey.

It was her. He was sure of it. She was sitting on the bench outside the supermarket. That bench. The same bloody supermarket. Seb was rooted to the spot, staring at her as she sat, slightly huddled, smoking a cigarette. She looked frail, smaller than he remembered, and was wearing a thin, brightly patterned dress, mostly red, with red high-heeled sling-back shoes, her skin pale, longish hair blowing in front of her face. She was chewing her lip, looking nervously to her right and left. Agitated, maybe even scared. Pretty, though. Then she looked across the road, straight at him.

Caught. Red-handed. Red-faced, more like, as he felt himself blushing. He glanced away and then looked back.

The girl, Janey, was stubbing out her cigarette on the pavement and looked like she was getting ready to leave. Maybe it was the fact that he'd found someone, even if it wasn't the person he was looking for, that made him do it. He never did work it out, but the next thing he knew he was dodging through the cars to the other side of the street. And then there he was, standing in front of her, tongue in a knot.

'What?'

'You're, um, y'know, Janey, aren't you?'

'Do I know you?'

'Sort of.' Seb caught a slight scent of the girl's perfume – delicate, flowery, warm – and just for a moment was right there, back in the room with her.

'Look, I gotta go, really . . . not supposed to be here . . . '

'Could we just talk for a couple of minutes?'

''Fraid not. If I'm seen out here, I'm in trouble.'

'I could pay . . . ' Seb stopped. He had *not* wanted to say that. That was so out of order. Then he saw her rubbing her arm and noticed a large, fading bruise.

'Fuck you.' It was said with cold anger.

'I didn't mean . . . '

'Just leave me alone, will you? I've *really* gotta go.' Head down, her eyes darted around as she spoke. 'Shit!'

'What's the matter?' Seb glanced the way she was looking; who had she seen? Zack? There was no one he recognised anywhere on the street and when he looked back the girl had gone. Feeling slightly sick, he frantically searched the street before seeing a flash of red through the supermarket windows and realising she'd run off down a narrow alleyway that led off the street. Having found her one moment he wasn't about to lose her the next.

By the time he'd rounded the corner, Janey was right at the other end of the alley and turning left. Seb wasn't sure if he could hear someone calling out behind him, but he reckoned it would be wiser not to stick around to find out. So he legged it too.

Janey was heading up a small side street towards the bustle of a main road. Long Acre? Probably, if the map in his head was accurate. Seb saw her skid to a momentary halt on the kerb, then launch herself across the road, a car narrowly missing her. Brakes squealed, horns sounded and, as he ran, Seb waited for the dull crunch of plastic bumpers hitting expensive tail-light clusters. It didn't happen. The driver of the car that had so nearly hit Janey was still as white as a sheet, shaking a fist and yelling soundlessly at her back as Seb followed her across the road. How desperate did you have to be to take risks like that? If he ever caught up with her he might find out.

He could see her dodging through the mid-afternoon tourist herds, weaving this way and that, and then she veered off to the left. By the time he reached the passageway she'd gone, was nowhere to be seen. It was another of those *X-Files* moments, as there was no way she could've reached the end of the passage and got out of sight before he'd got there. She wasn't that far in front. But people didn't just disappear into thin air in real life.

Confused, Seb started to run, to get to the other end and check whether she really had managed to move so fast, when he caught a glimpse of red out of the corner of his eye. He stopped and looked back. Gone. But he was sure he'd seen her dress. She must've slipped into the restaurant he'd just gone past, obviously hoping he'd simply carry on running. He walked back and pushed open the wide glass door.

Inside, it was air-conditioned and he immediately felt the sweat cool on him, making him shiver involuntarily. This time in the afternoon there were only a few late-lunch stragglers, well into their brandies, and nobody was at the front desk. To one side were swing doors behind which he could see the kitchens, and to the other a staircase leading to the basement. A lit sign said that down there he'd find the bar and the toilets. Seb took the stairs, two at a time.

At the bottom, to his right, was the bar. Low-lit, almost empty. He looked in and couldn't see any sign of Janey; behind him he heard a door open slightly. Quickly he moved into the shadows by a cigarette machine and waited. The door to the Ladies opened a bit more, cold white light spilling on to the small corridor, and then Janey came out. The one place she didn't look was where Seb was standing.

'I just want to talk,' he said, moving into the light. 'That's all.'

Janey looked at him. 'Who *are* you . . . *why* are you following me?'

'Like I said, I just want to talk.'

'What about?'

That stopped him. What did he want to talk to her about? He had no idea, but he needed to buy some time to think of a good enough reason or she was going to be out of there.

'D'you want a drink?' Seb jerked a thumb in the direction of the bar. 'Zack's not going to find you in here.'

'Zack? You know him? Oh my God . . . I am *so* in trouble!' Janey seemed to crumple like tissue paper in front of him, shrinking back against the wall, as if waiting for a blow she knew was going to come her way, sooner or later.

'He's not a mate or anything. I only know him cos he beat me up after . . . well, he did me over, took all the money I had on me.' Seb reached out, beckoning. 'Come on, let me buy you a drink . . . '

'I remember you.' Janey was looking at him in a different way now. 'I remember him talking about the kicking he gave you.'

Seb didn't know how he felt. Nervous. Embarrassed. Foolish. Even angry. Mostly confused. What the hell was he doing here with this girl, what good was this going to do either of them? What could he say to her that would make anything better, that would change what had happened? A small voice in the bleakness of his head whispered that apologising for using her might make him feel slightly better, which was probably as good as it was ever going to get. It was an odd, perplexing thought, but under the circumstances it kind of made some sort of sense.

'Sorry,' he said, for the second time that day, but this time he actually meant it.

'What for?'

'Look, can we sit down?'

Janey chewed her lip, then nodded slightly. 'I need a bloody drink to face going back . . . OK, a quick one.'

'What d'you want?'

'Vodka tonic?'

'At the bar?'

'I'd prefer somewhere at the side, just in case.'

Seb nodded, watching her go and sit over in the corner furthest away from the entrance. She seemed so insubstantial, almost a ghost in the subdued light, a tiny, fleeting image at the back of the room that he felt might not be there if he turned away and then looked back again. And she could, of course, still run away. He moved round the bar to keep her in sight, ordering a couple of overpriced drinks from a bored waiter, as he stared at Janey.

Just like before in the street, outside the supermarket, she looked up, straight at him, knowing in that psychic way people often do that she was being observed. This time, though, he didn't blush and look away. He smiled back at her, watching her sit, still as a sculpture, frowning slightly. Waiting.

CHAPTER 15

OK, THEY'D HAD SEX. ONCE. BUT SEB WOULDN'T classify Janey as someone he knew. And here he was, chasing her down, demanding to have a conversation with her when he should be out trying to find Jay Brill. Except instead of talking he offered her a cigarette, lit it, asked if she wanted some peanuts, got them. Lit his own fag. Took a drink. Smiled. Anything but talk.

'What's your name, then?'

'Ah, Seb . . . Seb Mitchell. What's yours?'

'Ella Timmis.'

'Ella?' Seb frowned. 'But I thought . . . '

'I'm Ella *Jane*, the name on the card's something Zack dreamt up.'

'Oh . . . ' He was momentarily taken aback. A name was just a label, but people kind of became what they were called, looked like that's who they should be. This girl had been Janey, looked like a Janey. And now she was Ella. Had that changed her, made her a different person? How would he know.

'What did you say sorry for?'

'Yeah . . . right, why *did* I do that?' Seb ran his fingers through his hair, looking away distractedly. 'That day . . . Jesus. Look, I'd had a bitch of a day that day. Like, it kind of ended up being the worst day of my life. I didn't give a shit about anyone or anything and I did a load of things that I'm not, you know, proud of. OK?'

'So why say sorry to me?'

'For, you know . . . '

'Doing the business?'

'Yeah. Maybe.'

'You're weird.' Ella stubbed out her cigarette, dismissive. 'You rang the number, no one made you do it.'

Seb didn't say anything for some time. He thought about how he felt, about what she'd said, about what *he* really wanted to say.

'Apart from one other person, who I can't find, nobody else but me knows everything that went down that day,' he said, finally breaking his silence. 'When I saw you on that bench, it was a shock. It brought everything back, and I suppose, you know, I need to hear myself tell the whole story, explain myself to someone. I know it sounds fucked up, but I was totally hell-bent that day . . . I was boozing, thieving, everything . . . '

'Whoring.'

'Yeah. But you know, like if you're gonna crash and burn? You may as well properly do it in style.'

'Sounds about right. What went wrong?'

'I nearly died.'

Seb told her everything, from getting up to coming to in hospital four days later. Everything, including all his dodgy dealings with Martin, but minus the stuff about him beginning to believe there'd been a real, live angel looking out for him. Even he didn't know how he felt about those ideas, and he suspected Ella thought he was enough of a flake as it was. She watched him as he talked, finishing her drink, then chewing the ice cubes. Taking it all in, making no comments, just letting him download.

It didn't take that long, but he felt a huge sense of relief when he'd finished. Now somebody else knew, he wasn't alone any more.

'Your turn.'

'S'cuse me?'

'You know everything about me and I don't know a damn thing about you.'

'What's to tell?' Ella looked away.

'Tell me anything.'

'I'm a fucking cliché, Seb . . . nothing interesting to tell. I'm nothing special.' She looked back at him, sad, tired, resigned. 'Like that song says, I got caught in a trap and I can't walk out . . . something like that.'

'Elvis . . . *Suspicious Minds*.'

'Eh?'

'That song, it's by Elvis. My, um, my mum likes it.'

'Right . . . '

Seb saw Ella almost smile. 'What?'

'Nothing.' Her face blanked again.

'She plays the bloody CDs all the time, 'cept when my dad's around.'

'You don't have to make excuses.'

Seb didn't know why he felt he was being judged, why he assumed she was coming to unjustified conclusions about him and the way he lived; he just did. It made him uneasy, made him want to say that whatever she was thinking about him, it wasn't his fault. But that sounded whiney and pathetic. Maybe he should just give up, now he'd said his piece, and get on with what he was supposed to be doing. Maybe that was it for both of them. Except that neither of them seemed to be in any kind of hurry to leave.

'How did you get caught?'

'Caught?'

'In the trap. Can't walk out.'

'I ran away, but didn't look where I was going . . . '

She'd been born and brought up in some piece-of-shit sink estate in loose orbit in the wastelands east of the M25. A soulless place, she said, that was just there. It had schools, shops, houses and everything. It had people who had jobs, but no careers, it had children, fast-food joints, multiplexes, shopping malls and supermarkets, but no community. It had bricks and mortar, but it didn't have a heart and if you came from there, you never felt like you had a future. It was a place built to leave.

Her mother had done just that, leaving when Ella was twelve. She'd bunked off with some bloke called Terry she'd met on the night shift at the factory where she worked as a supervisor; they'd gone to live in Spain. Leaving Ella and her older brother, Duncan, behind with their dad.

It'd been OK for a bit. Then Duncan started getting into trouble and, once he reached eighteen, got put away for it. Not long after that, her dad began to drink. Why not, he'd said, nothing was going to get any better. And Jesus was he right about that. Their situation seemed designed to breed tension, despair and frustration, that was what it was like in her house, anyway. She spent most of her time trying to keep out of her dad's way. He spent most of his getting pissed.

She left the day after he'd hit her. Gave her a black eye,

bruises everywhere. And that was it. She'd ignored the verbal abuse, zoned it out, mostly, but when he came at her in a mad drunken rage he'd scared the shit out of her. Next time, she'd thought, she could end up dead. You read about things like that in the papers.

Ella knew her dad didn't mean it, wasn't truly bad. But sticking around any longer seemed, at the time, too big a risk to take. Looking back, coming up to town hadn't been the most sensible thing she'd ever done; she should've gone and stayed with a friend and sorted out what to do later. But she was eighteen, who planned things?

'I had about £100 on me, all my savings. Thought I'd find somewhere to stay for a couple of nights, like a cheap hotel? Get a job in a shop or something and find a flat. Easy.'

'What happened?'

'Zack happened.'

'How d'you mean?'

'People like him are always on the lookout for people like me. We're easy meat. I was on my own in some bar in Soho . . . thought I knew my way round, thought I was cool. I'd had a few drinks, like you do, and I was asking anyone who'd listen if they knew anywhere I could stay. I couldn't have made it easier for him if I'd tried.'

'How long ago?'

'Just two months . . . '

The whole time she'd been talking, Ella hadn't looked at Seb, had stared at the table top, hair hanging in front of her face. Hiding in the open. Now she lifted her head. 'Can I have another ciggie?'

Seb gave her his packet and the lighter. Something told

him – a pleading look in her eyes? – that this was where the story should end. Please. Unlike him, maybe Ella didn't need to unload everything. Too painful. She didn't need anyone else to know, but for some reason she'd trusted him with more than she'd really wanted to say. In the silence he realised she was absentmindedly stroking the bruise on her arm again.

'Did he do that?'

'Do what?'

'Zack. Did he hit you?'

'Smack his bitch up? Yeah. Makes my dad look like a bloody saint.'

'What, um . . . why d'you, like . . . '

'Why do I stay?'

Seb nodded.

'Dickhead.' Cold, voice raised. Angry. 'Cos I bloody *love* what I do, don't I. I'm a fucking tart with a heart – why d'you think I stay, shit-for-brains? He won't let me fucking go, OK?'

Behind him Seb heard the barman cough. A warning? He checked his watch. Jeez, they'd been in the place for almost two hours. It was nearly five o'clock and he was suddenly aware that a few people had drifted into the bar while they'd been talking. The first of the evening crowd.

'What's the time?' Ella grabbed his wrist, pulling it towards her and squinting in the low light. 'Shit!'

She got up, hitting the table between them with her knees and knocking over their glasses. As he leant over to pick them up before they fell on to the floor, Ella ran past him and made for the stairs. Seb pushed his chair back, grabbed his backpack and ran after her.

He caught her up by the front door, where she'd been

stopped by a snotty and very suspicious bloke with spiky, dyed blond hair, tinted glasses and wearing a suit with too many buttons. Must be the bloke in charge of the place. He was barring Ella's way and Seb could tell she was about to lose it, big time.

'She's with me.' He skirted past the man, took Ella by the hand and pushed open the door with his shoulder. 'We're late for an appointment – gotta go!'

Out in the passageway it was all Seb could do to keep a hold of Ella, to stop her from wrenching herself away and disappearing again. She was desperate, close to tears, babbling, and Seb could see the man in the restaurant watching them.

'Don't run . . . don't run, we can sort this out.'

'He's gonna use me as a fucking *ashtray*!'

'No, no he won't.'

'I'm in *so* much trouble! You *bastard*, why couldn't you just leave me alone? I didn't need you turning up in my life!'

'I can help.' Seb tried to move them both down the passage, away from prying eyes, as he spoke. 'Let me help, Ella.'

'No bloody thanks!' She yanked her hand away and Seb thought she'd make a run for it, but she just stood where she was, her eyes wide, her chin trembling, a single tear running down her cheek. 'Oh God, oh God, oh God . . . he's gonna kill me when he finds me, he's gonna fucking *kill* me . . . '

It was a statement of fact, lacking any exaggeration or embellishment, and Seb suddenly felt completely responsible and totally out of his depth. He'd really meant it when he said he wanted to help; he wanted her to let him, but what could he actually do? She was right, it was his fault she was in so much trouble, and he knew she wasn't kidding because he had personal experience of what an evil shit Zack was. He could truly believe he'd use her as an ashtray, and worse. He had to think of something.

Ella, almost visibly shrinking in front of him, like she was trying to sink into the pavement, still hadn't said anything else, as if that was it, she'd given up all hope and was just waiting to be put out of her misery.

Seb took her hand again and this time she didn't resist. It was a fairly warm afternoon, but she felt cold. Fear? Could fear do that to you? He had no idea. Face it, he had no idea about anything. He was lost, adrift in shark-infested waters, up Shit Creek without a paddle in sight. Any moment now Zack, or someone else who knew Ella, could simply turn a corner and see them both and the game would be well and truly up.

Even if he got her off the street, took her to another bar or pub or restaurant, what then? They couldn't stay anywhere for ever, everywhere closed eventually. And then something mad occurred to him. There was somewhere they could stay. He undid the sweatshirt he had tied round his waist, pulled Ella towards him and wrapped it round her shoulders.

'I, um, I've got an idea,' he said.

CHAPTER 16

USHING THROUGH THE BEGINNINGS OF THE rush-hour crowds, Seb guided Ella down towards the far side of the Covent Garden Piazza. She was like a zombie, going wherever he took her, all the fight gone. It gave Seb the chance actually to think about what he was doing. Not such a bad idea, when you were faced with the kind of dilemma he had.

On the one hand, how could he possibly let her go back? On the other hand, what did he know about her? Absolutely nothing, except what she'd told him. And who's to say she was telling the truth? She could, for all he knew, be a thieving, lying, schizoid junkie. Just the sort of person you wanted to take home to meet your mum, which, when you came down to it, was his Great Idea. Take her home, let her stay. Simple.

Seb glanced back at the girl he was pulling behind him. Did she want to get out of her life and go where he was taking her, into the unknown? You'd think so, but if he'd learnt one thing in his life it was that it was stupid to assume anything. Sod's Law, you'd a better than average chance of being wrong. Better to find out for sure. He stopped walking and stepped off the pavement, taking Ella with him into the doorway of a shop that had gone out of business. They stood in this calm space, on a carpet of yesterday's news, junk food junk and fag ends.

'Do you want to get out of here?'

'What?' Ella looked confused, like Seb was talking a foreign language.

'My idea, right? My idea is to take you back to mine, you can stay there for a few days, you know, till we sort something out. Zack'll never find you. What d'you think? There's no point in going on if you don't want to.'

'Your house?'

'Yeah.'

Silence. She looked away, chewing gum. Then stared at him, sideways, eyes narrowed. 'Why would you do that? What's in it for you – why're you suddenly coming on like a big knight, all in shining armour?'

'I've no bloody idea, Ella, except . . . except I can't just let you walk off and end up with Zack again.'

'Well, who's a lucky girl to have a guardian angel, then?'

It was like when you're on your Walkman and someone creeps up and yanks the earphones out for a laugh. One moment you're connected to the sounds completely surrounding your head, the next they're gone. Seb felt totally distanced from what was happening, shifted, as if everything around him had been deadened.

Why was she talking about guardian angels?

'Too weird, too bloody weird.'

'What?' Ella moved nearer the street.

Seb suddenly realised he'd been talking out loud and he could feel himself blushing. 'All I'm trying to do is help!'

'Look, I didn't mean . . . sorry . . . '

'Yeah, me too,' Seb sighed.

'Like, as in sorry you ever talked to me?'

'No, Ella, like sorry I got you into trouble, sorry all I've got is a crap idea to do something about it, all right?' Seb pushed rubbish around with the toe of his shoe. 'Why, um . . . why did you call me a guardian angel?'

'No reason.'

'OK.'

'OK? OK *what*?' Ella looked like she was ready to punch something. 'Look, why *should* I trust you, or you me, for that matter? This is *so* screwed up, I can't believe it. Go *home* with you – who the fuck are you anyway? Just some bloke. And I'm just some girl, one you paid for, right, so why don't we leave it at that? Eh?'

Seb looked at her, waiting to see if there were any more. 'Is that what you want?'

'How do I know?' Ella's shoulders slumped. 'I don't bloody *know* what I want, do I?'

'Listen . . . ' Seb offered Ella a cigarette, but she waved the packet away, ' . . . right now I've got to trust you *totally* as much as you've got to trust me. We're in the same boat, both of us, yeah?'

Seb saw a slight, almost imperceptible nod of agreement. An improvement. 'Give me a break, then.'

'OK, but . . . ' Ella looked down, smoothing a crease out of her thin dress. 'This is all I've got to wear.'

'Remember I told you about nicking that money off that woman?' Another nod. 'Cos I've still got quite a bit left. Couldn't spend any more of it after what happened, didn't seem right for some reason, but I didn't know what to do with it.'

'And?'

'And I thought I could buy you some clothes . . . like a disguise? In case Zack was out looking for you and spotted us on the way to the tube? Thought that was an OK thing to

134

do with the money. This is the way to Covent Garden market, where I was taking you, before . . . '

'Before we stopped to have a shit-fit with each other.'

'Are we gonna do this or what?' Seb looked at his watch. 'Cos we haven't got all day.'

'I still don't understand why you're bloody doing this.'

'Neither do I . . . '

A quick stop at a cashpoint resulted in another argument, at the end of which Seb found himself agreeing that Ella was going to pay him back for everything, as soon as she got a job. Then he finally took her into the market. It was coming to the end of the trading day and some of the stalls were beginning to pack up, but it was still pretty buzzy, a bit like Seb imagined a market in somewhere like Cairo must be, without the goats and the smell of drains. Actually, he thought as he watched her try on clothes, probably nothing like Cairo at all.

He ended up buying her jeans, shoes, a top, a jacket, a bag and something to clip her hair up with. Then he bought them each a pair of sunglasses. With every item Ella finally chose and put on she seemed to become somehow stronger, as if she was not just changing clothes but changing into a different person. It was when she wound her hair high up on her neck, fixing it with the fake tortoiseshell clip, and put on the sunglasses, that Seb knew he'd never have recognised her if she'd looked like that outside the supermarket.

The scared, twitched person who'd agreed to have a drink with him in the bar had retreated under the protective shell of a new look. Amazing what clothes could do. All he had to do now was get her past anyone looking for her, get on to the tube and go home.

His final purchase for her in the market was a baseball cap, and as they walked out he put on his shades as well, catching sight of the two of them in a shop window. Two people, friends, out shopping. That's what they looked like, but it was just an act and they were playing their parts as if their lives depended on it. So, he wondered as they went out into the Piazza, does a lie become true if you say it's the truth often enough?

And if you believed in something – *really, really believed*, say in like angels – did that make them real . . .

Oddly, Seb was more nervous now they were making their way towards the tube than he had been getting to the market. He'd had plenty of time to imagine what would happen if Zack recognised Ella, and to wonder what he'd do if things got rough.

Would anyone help them? Probably not. He'd seen stuff happen before where something kicked off and everyone disappeared, himself included, when it looked like they might have to get involved. There was a fascination in watching a fight, witnessing some in-yer-face argument that was usually the inevitable outcome of too much drinking, that drew you like a magnet. But, for Seb, the fascination soon turned to a sudden need to be somewhere else if the violence looked like it was coming his way.

Walking next to him, holding on to his arm like a clamp, Ella was looking straight ahead. He, on the other hand, was scanning the street in front of him like he were a front-line scout and they were in a war zone. Not so far from the truth. There were victims everywhere, lying slumped in heaps, covered in rags and as still as corpses; others, like war-wounded, sat waiting for help to arrive, hands out for something to see them through till it did.

'Nearly there.'

'What?' Ella jumped as Seb spoke. So nervous, both of them.

'I just said we're nearly at the station, nearly there.'

'Oh . . . yeah . . . '

'You OK?'

'Don't ask stupid questions.'

'Sorry.'

'And *stop* saying sorry.'

'Fine, fine . . . ' Seb was about to tell her to calm down when a figure lurched out of an alleyway and loomed right in front of them. Before he had a chance to focus properly, adrenaline hit his system like an electric shock, his ears sang with the bloodrush and his heart pounded. His mouth went dry. Beside him, Ella gasped and held on even tighter.

'Twenny pee for a cuppa tea, eh? Jus' a li'l twenny pee, boss!'

The sun was by now quite low, and wearing cheap sunglasses just obscured anything or anybody even slightly in the shadows. All Seb could see was a dark shape, but there was something about the ragged bloke weaving in front of him, his slurred voice catching Seb's attention and stopping him from walking on. He took off his sunglasses. 'Billy?'

'You know him?' Ella's grip relaxed slightly.

'Sort of . . . is that you Billy?'

'Billy, yeah.' He put his hand out, smiling. 'You got a li'l something for good ole Billy?'

'Who is he?'

'The guy I told you about . . . the one who drew the picture for me.' Seb took out all the change he had in his pocket, about a fiver's worth, and held it out, aware that, while there were quite a few people about, no one was paying them any attention.

'Ta, boss, thanks very much, very kind.'

Seb watched Billy count the money, swaying slightly from side to side as he did. He felt a deep, empty sadness; he'd kind of imagined, in his head, that Billy was one of those people who lived on the edge out of choice and not because booze, drugs or both kept him there. He knew that Billy had let too many chances go, but why did he have to be making his bad luck worse?

'See you, Billy.' Seb reached out and squeezed the man's shoulder.

'Gaw' bless you, boss.'

'You're just gonna give him money so he can get more pissed and leave him here?' Ella had let go of Seb's arm and was frowning at him.

'Ella . . . '

'How can you just walk away? Is he worth less than me?'

'It's not like that.'

Billy was still counting the money and didn't seem to be aware they were still there.

'What *is* it like then?' She wasn't shouting, but he could tell she was angry. 'Have you got some fucking scale for people who are worth saving or something?'

'Can we do this some other time?' Seb felt drained and the last thing he wanted right now was a scene.

Ella didn't say anything, and Seb couldn't tell what she was thinking, or figure out what she might do next. Then he saw a tear roll down her cheek, followed by a second. 'It's not bloody fair, is it?'

Seb watched her wipe her cheek, sniffing. He handed her

a reasonably new tissue. 'No.'

She took the tissue and blew her nose. 'Let's go, OK?'

They walked down the street in silence, the tube station now only a couple of hundred metres away. Seb glanced back and couldn't see Billy any more.

CHAPTER 17

QUEUEING FOR A TICKET FOR ELLA, BECAUSE none of the machines was giving change, Seb kept glancing over his shoulder. Checking. Useless really, cos he had no idea who, apart from Zack, might be looking for her, but it was becoming a habit. The concourse was filling up, crowds streaming through the automatic barriers to the Northern and Piccadilly lines, and they'd soon be able to lose themselves amongst them. There was safety in numbers, they said. He hoped they were right.

Still wearing her baseball cap and sunglasses, Ella was sticking to him like a shadow, silent and behind him whenever he turned. She was going through moods so fast he could hardly keep up, but then who could blame her. She must be pretty spooked by what had happened in the last few hours. Not to mention what lay ahead.

'Which line?'

'Sorry?'

'Which line are we taking?'

'Northern, Barnet branch . . . these escalators right here.' Seb gave Ella her ticket and guided her through the barriers, into the river of people and on to the moving steps. They stood, letting the keen, the eager and the late dive past them like lemmings, and he could feel her radiating anxiety.

'Don't you like the tube, Ella?'

'No.'

'Right.'

'All these thousands of people underground.' Ella's eyes flicked left and right. 'In tunnels. Bloody madness.'

'Tunnels?' Seb wondered what she was on about.

'It's like, closing in . . . pressing down?'

'You claustrophobic?'

'You psychic?'

It wasn't a question requiring an answer, so he didn't bother replying. Instead, he checked the indicator and, seeing that they'd have to wait for a few minutes for a Barnet branch train, eased them both along the platform to stand in one particular spot.

'Why've we stopped here?'

'Um . . . no reason.'

'I hate this.'

'I realise . . . I'd've suggested the bus if I'd known . . . why didn't you say?'

Silence.

'It won't take long, you know, the journey?'

'I'm fine.'

The two of them stood in silence, staring at the massive, grainy images and huge type in the posters on the other side of the track, not reading, not really seeing what they were looking at. Seb glanced at Ella, her eyes hardly blinking behind the sunglasses, then he looked down at the train tracks and saw the tiny black scurry of a tube mouse darting from concrete pillar to discarded food wrapper.

He was about to point it out to Ella but then thought better of it. Knowing his luck she'd be even more frightened of mice than she was of being on the tube, and that would really put the icing on the cake. Then he felt Ella nudge him.

'What?'

'Look at that.'

'At what?' Seb looked at Ella.

'Down there, a mouse.'

'Yeah, cool aren't they?'

'As long as they're down there . . . I'd be screaming my face off if it was up on the platform.'

'Right . . . ' Seb nodded to himself, wondering what the reaction would've been if *he'd* pointed out the mouse. You never could tell, could you.

'How much longer . . . ?'

Seb caught the edge in her voice; he'd momentarily forgotten what was happening, lost in the auto-pilot mode brought on by doing something you've done so many times. He quickly scanned the densely packed platform. No vicious bastards pushing their way towards them that he could see. Then he glanced up at the destination indicator. 'Train'll be here in two minutes.'

There was an odd ebb and flow to the underground, platforms filling up and emptying, like watching the sea run up and down a beach. An almost empty Edgware train came into the station and most of the people waiting surged on to it like they were being sucked in; the doors closed and, moving off slowly, the train appeared to pull a trickle of people out of the tunnels as it went. Before the platform had time to become uncomfortably crowded again the Barnet train arrived, stopping with the single door at the end of a carriage right opposite Seb and Ella.

Seeing there were a couple of empty seats facing the platform, Seb urged Ella through the door as soon as it opened and they got them. He sat back and breathed out, loudly; it was a relief to finally be getting away from what he'd come to think of as the danger zone.

'How many stops?'

'A few . . . ' Seb looked up at the map opposite and counted the stations. 'Eleven,' he said, as the doors closed and the train began to move.

'Will it take long?'

Seb didn't reply. He couldn't. Standing on the platform, looking right at him, was Jay Brill. Wasn't it?

Seb was beyond shocked, heart pounding, palms hot and sweaty as he gripped the plastic armrests, holding on for dear life as if letting go would allow him to be torn out of his seat and flung away.

Wearing a white T-shirt and a grey zip-up jacket, his face looking exactly like the sketch Billy Swift had done, Jay Brill had only been fifteen metres from where he and Ella had been standing. Seb was dumbstruck, unable to move, speak or think. The man was right there in front of him, standing outside the train on the platform!

He was smiling, holding a single white flower with a thick, green stem, wrapped in cellophane, eyes now flicking left and right as the train began to speed up. Seb felt himself jerk as his head tried to work out what to make his body do – reach up and pull the communication cord? Yell? Wave? Go mental and try and slide the door back and get back out on to the platform?

'Seb?'

The man he was sure was Jay Brill, the person he'd almost begun to believe didn't exist, was sort of looking Seb's way again and, as he disappeared from view, seemed like he was about to wave. And then he was gone.

Seb felt cold, weighted down, as if gravity was crushing him; there was nothing he could do now, no point in getting out at the next station and going back, because the man wouldn't be waiting. He'd lost him. There, and then gone, like he'd never even been there.

'*Seb!*' A shout in his ear brought him back.

'Fuck . . . ' A whisper was all he could manage.

'What's the matter?'

'That man.'

'What man?'

'The one on the platform, with the flower.'

'What about him?'

'Did you see him?'

'Yeah, kind of, why?'

'I've been looking for him . . . I needed to find him.' Seb leant forward, his head in his hands, and then he sat back. He was shaking. He actually felt like crying. 'He was just fucking *there* . . . just there.'

'Who is he?'

Now there was a question.

Who was he? That was the whole damn point, wasn't it, because he didn't bloody know . . . needed to find the man to find out. And he'd been there, just out of reach. He'd bloody been there, almost within reach, standing just up the platform, but Seb hadn't spotted him. He'd been looking for Zack, not Jay Brill.

But what was he doing there? Was he still watching over him?

'Seb . . . are you OK?'

'Yeah . . . ' Seb saw the worried look in Ella's face and knew he owed her some sort of explanation for his weird behaviour. Could also be that telling her all about the whole angel thing might help sort it out in his head. Or convince him that he was going certifiably insane. He glanced around; a crowded tube was probably not the best place to start this whole conversation off. 'Look, just wait till we get off the train and I'll tell you everything . . .'

'OK, it's just that you looked like you were going to have a heart attack.' Ella squeezed his hand.

'What?' Seb frowned, then couldn't help laughing. 'Nothing that dramatic.'

They were sitting on a low wall, opposite a funky old cinema, a single-screen place that seemed to specialise in showing retro movies and foreign stuff with subtitles. Seb had now told Ella the whole Jay Brill story, about how someone he'd never met had saved his life, even though the guy appeared to have been following him all that day and knew all about the bad crap he'd been up to. And he'd told her about Mrs Sanders calling Jay his 'guardian angel', how he'd kind of 'tested' the theory and, since then, hadn't been able to get the weird thought that somehow Jay might be an angel out of his head.

'D'you, um, d'you believe in angels, Ella?'

'Never thought about it much.'

'Me either.'

'Bit like ghosts, aren't they . . . I mean, people with wings, what's that all about?'

'I dunno – I mean, what if it's true, what if we *do* have someone looking out for us?'

'Yeah, well who's the lucky one, cos mine's been bugger all use.'

'And mine could be just some bloke.' Seb got up and stretched; he still felt wired after what had happened on the tube. He was emotionally shredded.

'You reckon that was him then,' Ella stood up too, 'you know, the man with the flower?'

'Did you get a good look at him?'

'Sort of.'

'Well, try and remember his face and I'll show you the drawing that guy Billy did when we get home.'

'Christ!' Ella sat down on the wall again.

'What's the matter?'

'I'd kind of forgotten we were going to your house . . . what the bloody hell's your mum gonna say when you pitch up with me in tow? How's *that* gonna work, Seb?'

'I, um . . . '

'Seb! Look, what happens if everything really falls apart and I'm stuck out in the middle of nowhere with nowhere to go?'

'It'll be fine.'

'You always waltzing in with tarts you've only just met?'

'My parents won't know we've only just met . . . they won't know where you've been, what you've had to do.' Seb looked at Ella, chewing her lip, looking back up at him: small, exposed, like an island in the calm eye of a storm, waiting for disaster. 'And anyway, my mum'll be delighted.'

'Your mum? Why?'

'Ever since Shona dumped me? She's been asking about whether I've got another girlfriend, or "someone special", as she puts it.'

'Have you?'

'No.'

'Why not?'

Seb shrugged. 'Had a lot of other stuff on my mind . . .

hadn't really thought about it. Anyway, she'll just assume we're an item, cos that's what she wants – me sorted and back to "normal",' he made inverted comma marks with his fingers, 'and whatever she tells my old man he'll take for gospel. You'll see, there won't be a problem.'

'What if there is?'

'There won't be . . . I know my mum, she likes everything to be OK, she doesn't want to worry; if I've got a new girlfriend she doesn't have to worry about me *not* having one.'

'Mums, eh?' Ella stared back down the street towards the tube station.

'Sorry.'

'Don't fucking say you're sorry.' Ella kept looking away. 'It's not your fault you've got a mum who didn't piss off and leave you.'

'It's a habit, like the cigs . . . I'm trying to give it up – shall we go?'

'Aren't you gonna ring or anything? Let her know you're bringing someone back?'

'She'd definitely think I was up to no good if I did that. Far too thoughtful.'

Ella grinned and stood up. 'OK, let's go.'

They'd only walked a few metres when Ella stopped. Seb turned back.

'What's up?'

'So I'm staying with you, in your room.' It was a statement of fact.

'Kinda gotta, if we're an item.'

Ella stood, eyes narrowed, one hand on her hip, observing Seb from a metre or so away, glancing to the side and looking back at him. Lips slightly curled.

'No look, don't get me wrong – you get the bed, I take

147

the floor, always the plan, OK?' Seb nodded at Ella. No response. 'C'mon, stop looking at me like that.'

'Like what, Seb?'

'Like I'm something got stuck on your damn shoe.'

'Your interpretation. I'm just a mirror.'

'Ferchristsake Ella, gimme a break!'

'Just kidding, I believe you. But this is just so fucking strange . . . you don't know who the hell I am, all you do know about me isn't very good and here you are, some weirdo who thinks he's seen an *angel*, taking me back to meet the parents!'

'You think I'm a weirdo?'

'I didn't mean it like that – give *me* a break, Seb . . . who the hell am I s'posed to be when the front door opens and there's your mum? What am I doing, how long am I staying? What's my fucking *name*?'

'Look, just chill a bit.' Seb held her hand, tight. She gripped back, hard, and then let go.

'Just chill?'

'Yeah, things'll work out, Ella, especially if we don't say too much.'

'What d'you mean?'

'With my parents? It's always been the more I made up stuff, the bigger the lie, the more chance I'd get caught out. Keep it simple. You're Ella, your parents are away for a couple or so weeks and you don't like it in the house alone. I said you'd stay with me for a bit. Simple.'

'You really had all this worked out?'

'I wish.'

'Chancer.'

CHAPTER 18

RIGHT AFTER THEY'D TURNED INTO HIS ROAD, FOR a second Seb thought he saw someone a couple of hundred metres down, peering out from behind a hedge by one of the turnings that ran off it. Adam and Steve? God, he wished there were a part of his life where he wasn't always having to worry about being followed. He looked again and no one was there now. If anyone ever had been.

Even though it was going to be more than a bit nervewracking, he actually couldn't wait to get back home. He was fairly sure that, between them, they could pull the whole thing off; the cover story held together pretty well, no gaping holes, and he reckoned his mum would buy it like it came from M&S. And with things like that, where she went, his dad usually followed.

'Nice houses.' Ella broke the silence.

'Yeah.'

'You don't like them?'

'They're OK.'

'Better than some scabby estate. How long've you lived here?'

'All my life . . . we moved here when my older brother was about two.'

'We were always moving . . . '

'Cos of your dad's work?'

'Not really,' Ella laughed, sour. 'Keeping one step ahead of the rent man, that was my dad's job.'

'We're nearly there.' Seb was struck by the thing of how different two lives could be – two people, similar ages, from the same general part of the same country, and at no point did their experiences match. Like parallel lifelines, never meeting. Except theirs had.

They walked past the turning where Seb had thought he'd spotted Adam and/or Steve. No one to be seen. And then there they were, stopped at his gate. Number 75. He got his key out of his backpack and pushed the gate open.

'Come on then . . . '

Seb's mum had been in the kitchen having a cup of tea when they walked in. She had the radio on loud enough to cover up their entrance and had been having a sly fag. She was supposed to have given up months ago, although Seb had spotted the tell-tale signs and just kept his mouth shut. Surprised, embarrassed and then flustered by their sudden appearance, she fussed around the kitchen, her cup in one hand and not quite knowing what to do with the cigarette she was still holding in the other.

'Hi Ma – this is Ella, she's my, like, new girlfriend.'

'Hello Mrs Mitchell.' Ella did a small 'hi there' wave.

'Hello,' his mum kind of smiled. 'Nice to meet you, ah, Ella.' She held up the cigarette and looked at Seb. 'Bad day at work . . . you, um, won't, you know?'

'No, I won't,' Seb smiled back, trying to keep a reasonably straight face. 'Anyway, Ella's parents are away and . . . '

'You're going to stay there?' his mum interrupted, still nervous.

'Not really, more the other way round, she's . . . the house is kind of too empty, freaks her out with no one else there? I said it would be OK if she stayed here for a bit.'

'Hope you don't mind,' Ella smiled.

'Oh . . . right, yes, good idea – where have they gone?' Seb's mum stubbed out her cigarette.

'Gone? Thailand . . . for, like three weeks? They've always wanted to go.'

'Lovely . . . you're not a vegetarian or anything are you?'

'Me?' Ella looked at Seb and then back at his mum. 'No, why?'

'I had a girlfriend once who was a veggie.' Seb watched his mum clean up the crime scene by emptying the ashtray into the rubbish bin and then carefully scrubbing it under a running tap. 'It made mealtimes kind of interesting.'

'She was a vegan, Seb – what was it your dad called her? A food fascist, wasn't it? She wouldn't eat *anything*.'

'I eat everything, Mrs Mitchell.'

'Glad to hear it. See you for dinner, then . . . we're having curry.'

Once they'd got upstairs and he'd closed his bedroom door, Seb felt he could finally relax after being stretched like a guitar string for what seemed like the whole day. He wanted to burst into hysterical laughter, but was worried his mum would think he was laughing at her expense – which, to be fair, he would be a bit. And he wanted to grab Ella and yell, 'We did it!', but that wouldn't sound too good either and, anyway, Ella didn't look much like she wanted to do any leaping up and down.

'You OK? You did great down there – just totally seamless!'

Ella simply stood, slightly hunched, shaking her head, staring out of the window and holding a hand to her mouth.

'What is it?'

'Can't believe I'm here. Gonna wake up in a minute . . .'

'It's real, Ella.'

'No, it's not . . . it's gonna end sometime, in a couple of weeks or whatever.' Ella sniffed and shook herself back into shape, standing a little taller. 'It's not real, but it's a very nice dream.'

Before Seb could reply, there was a knock on his door and he heard his mum saying she had a couple of cups of tea for them. He opened the door to find she was holding a tray with a plate of biscuits on it as well.

'Oh, and before I forget, a friend of yours called earlier,' she said as she handed him the tray and started to go down the stairs.

'Who was it?'

'Oh, what was his name . . . I've got it written down somewhere – he didn't leave a number, said you'd know how to get in touch.'

'Was it, like, Adam or Steve?'

'No . . . oh God, I'm having one of those "senior moments" when your brain turns to rice pudding . . . Martin, that's it! Martin, he said his name was Martin.'

Seb closed the door and stood holding the tray. Bloody Martin. How the hell had he got his home number – was it a kind of 'I know where you live' threat? He was really going to have to do something other than turning off his mobile.

'Who's Martin?'

'What?'

'You don't seem too pleased he called.'

'I'm not, he's that slimeball I told you about, the one who's got it into his fucked-up head he wants me back doing stuff for him.'

'Haven't you told him to get lost?'

'Yeah.' Seb shook his head in disbelief at what had happened. 'I told him a couple of times.'

'So why's he calling?'

'I think that was his way of saying he doesn't take no for an answer.'

'And there was me thinking I was the one with all the problems.' Ella took a cup and a biscuit and sat down on the edge of the bed. 'I thought this was, like, a nice area.'

'What makes you think people don't do stuff in "nice" areas?' Seb put the tray on the carpet and went to look out of the window. 'I'll have to sort him out, once and for all.'

Ella was about to ask him something when she stopped and looked around the room, properly taking in where she was for the first time and seeing the huge work-in-progress leaning up against the wall to her right. Seb turned and saw her staring at Leonardo man, drawn into the intricate, multi-coloured patterns made by the silk threads, cup held halfway to her lips.

'D'you like it?'

'It's beautiful . . . what does it mean?'

'Depends where you look at it from. Stand up close and you get lost in the design and all you can see is detail; stand far enough back and . . . '

'You can see a man – two men.'

'Exactly.'

'Is it you?'

'Yeah, in a couple of ways.'

'How d'you mean?'

153

Seb walked over to the piece. 'It's kind of how I think, and at the same time it's what I am . . . that's the idea, anyway. It's like, everything you do is connected? And that you need to get further away from stuff to see what it means, cos the closer you are to things the more complicated they get. Does any of that make sense?'

'Yeah, makes perfect sense, from where I'm sitting.'

'And I've got to get this finished, get bloody Martin off my back and try to find Jay Brill.' Seb glanced at the pinboard. 'All at the same time.'

Ella followed Seb's glance and saw the drawing staring back at her in that uncanny way that it did. 'That him, the man with the flower on the tube?'

'D'you recognise him?'

Ella nodded.

'Yeah, that's Jay Brill. All I wanted to do was say thanks . . . he was standing just up from me on the same bloody platform – I could've done it right there and it would all be finished! Just thinking about it makes me crazy, it's so fucking frustrating.'

Ella grinned up at him. 'No one ever said it was supposed to be easy.'

'You sound like my dad . . . *please* don't do that.'

Dinner had its moments, but Seb's dad was in a pretty good mood because the agency had won a pitch and that, he said, meant steady work. There were a couple of awkward, searching questions from him about what Ella's parents did, but she dealt with them by giving simple answers and then turning the discussion round on itself by asking Seb's dad probing questions about his own work. A subject she'd obviously sussed he loved to talk about. Problem solved.

When the meal was over his mum had made coffee, while he and Ella cleared up; that job finished, they made their excuses and went back upstairs. After everything that had gone down since they'd met, everything they'd been through and said, there was suddenly an awkward atmosphere in the room, like neither of them knew what to do next.

Seb opened a window, lit a joss stick and offered Ella a cigarette. She took one and accepted a light. He lit another and stood by the window. She yawned. So did he. Both of them started to say something and neither of them got the sentence out.

'Are you kind of . . . ' Seb looked questioning.

'What?'

'You know, tired?'

'Kind of,' Ella nodded, looking away.

'Shall I . . . '

'Uh?'

'Shall I get you a towel and like show you where stuff is?'

'Yeah, thanks . . . that'd be great, Seb.'

By the time Ella came back to the bedroom, having taken a long, long shower, Seb had found a spare pillow, laid out his sleeping bag on a foam mat the other side of the room from his bed and got in, leaving just the bedside light on. He'd given her an XXL T-shirt to wear in bed, a joke present his brother had brought back from a trip to the States; it was massive on him and quite ridiculous on Ella, but something stopped him from commenting.

She got into bed, reaching over to turn the light out, and they both lay in the dark, listening to the night noises and the soft murmur of the TV programme his parents were watching downstairs. Their silence was like a physical thing in the room, but Seb, for one, couldn't think of what to say to break it.

'Seb?'

Finally, he thought. 'Yeah?'

'Thank you.'

'For what?'

'Oh, just everything.'

'No problem.'

'And, um . . . sorry.'

'Sorry?' Seb looked over at Ella's dark shape. 'What for?'

'Oh, just everything.'

'You got nothing to say sorry for, Ella . . . and anyway, if I'm supposed not to say sorry any more, neither are you.'

Silence again.

'Seb?'

'U-huh?'

'Really don't take this the wrong way, but . . . '

'But what?'

'Come here.'

'Ella, you don't have to . . . '

'I just need to *hold* someone, I just need to hold you, Seb. Please?'

Whichever way you looked at it, this was about as strange as it got. Confused? He was. The rational side of his head knew she didn't need some horny bloke groping her right now, knew that what she was asking for was a teddy bear substitute. The bloke side of things didn't really get it at all.

'Please?'

Not knowing what else to do, Seb got out of his sleeping bag and surreptitiously put on a pair of boxers before climbing under the duvet. She was cold, almost shivering, and he gathered the duvet around her, his arm outside the cover with her head on his shoulder.

'Thanks, Seb . . . '

'It's OK.'

She fell asleep within what seemed like seconds. He stayed awake for hours. He knew that because the red LEDs on his alarm clock kept blinking at him from across the room, a constant reminder that, although he felt totally done in, his brain was wired and wouldn't let him go to sleep. At 02:02 precisely, Seb sat up. Ella had rolled away and was curled up like a hamster and didn't move a muscle as he got out of bed.

'Bloody Martin,' he whispered to himself as he got dressed as quietly as he could, listening to the gentle rhythm of Ella's breathing. Picking up a couple of things from the floor, he left the room.

CHAPTER 19

SOME OF THE STREET LIGHTS WERE OUT ON THE road up to the High Street, pools of grey-black night lying between the stretches lit by the acid orange lamps. Who fixed these things? Seb couldn't remember ever seeing anyone – day or night – changing bulbs and stuff. One of life's many mysteries, almost up there with why you never saw baby pigeons. The things you thought about when you were trying not to think about what you were about to do.

Dressed in black jeans, a dark-grey hoody and black trainers, Seb had a black nylon bumbag slung over his shoulder and was now wishing he'd taken a baseball cap as well. Incognito was the word to live by on this little jaunt. There was pretty much no traffic, and in these back streets no people to see him either, but better safe than be spotted by anyone. One or two houses had a room with a light on, occasionally there was a TV on in a front room, the pulsating glow making it appear like it had a box full of squirming radioactive creatures in there, but most had blank eyes out to the world. Sensibly, most people weren't out trying to get a message through to some dozy sod who wouldn't listen.

Up on the High Street, things were a bit different. Even though it was closing in on 3am there were a few people out, some hanging around in a group by a bus stop, a couple of people, obviously the worse for wear, shouting obscenities at a cash machine and a few cars. No police though, as far as Seb could see. No police was good, as he didn't want to get pulled over, for whatever reason they might cook up, because he had a couple of cans of spray paint left over from Leonardo man, a pair of rubber gloves and a small MagLite in the bumbag.

He wasn't a tagger, but that would be seen as a writer's kit. He'd have some explaining to do if that lot was found and he really didn't need that level of hassle.

Getting off the main drag as fast as possible, Seb made his way over towards the old block of flats Martin used as a base and spent a few minutes in the doorway of a shop opposite checking them out. From where he was standing he could see the name on the outside, above the front entrance, and Denmore Court looked like it could well do with a lick of paint.

For the idea to work, he had to be able to get to the windows of the ground-floor flat where he'd been introduced to the wacky world of suburban drug dealing. This wasn't where Martin lived or anything, just where he did day-to-day business, and as he looked at the building Seb tried to remember as much as he could about the layout of the place so he'd be able to figure out which were the right windows.

Most likely, the red curtains would still be drawn so he wouldn't be able to see in to check, and he didn't want to get the wrong flat if he could help it. From what he could make out from where he was standing, there was an alleyway at the side of the building facing him that led round to the back, where, if he was right, he'd find the windows to the flat he wanted.

Checking the coast was clear, Seb slipped across the road and into the narrow alley; it was where the big, industrial-sized wheely bins for the flats were kept and it stank of old rubbish and cat piss. Walking as if the ground were covered in eggshells, which in places it actually was, Seb made his way past the bins and round to the back of the building. If the plan in his head was accurate, the place he wanted was on the next corner.

Before he went to find out he moved back into the alley, put the rubber gloves on, got out the two spray cans and took off his hoody; he then wiped the cans and wrapped the hoody round them and gave the bundle a vigorous shake. You could still hear the ball bearings rattle, but the thick cotton material had at least deadened some of the sound. While he did a quick check, scanning every window he could see, Seb put his hoody back on and the cans back in the bumbag and then scooted down to the next corner in a crouch, like he was expecting small arms fire to break out at any moment and spray the building with bullets.

Not a shot was fired. But, across the road, above one of the shops, a light turned on. Seb waited to see if anything else happened before he took a look at the room the other side of the glass. Nothing did, so he used the ledge to pull himself up and peered over the sill; the room's curtains had only been roughly drawn, so he could see in, but he found himself staring at the heavy-duty concertina security lattice that had been pulled across the two windows. Lucky he hadn't been looking to break in.

The room was dark, but he could see it was the right place. He could just make out the massive plasma TV, now just a blank screen, with Martin's chair opposite it. Taking a deep breath, Seb stood up, moved to the right-hand window and started spraying with a can of black paint, working his way over from right to left, first one window, then the next. When he'd finished he put down the can and took out the second one; going back to where he'd started he began spraying red paint inside the black outline he'd just done.

The aerosol hiss sounded so loud in the still night, like amplified FM static, but less than 45 seconds after he'd started spraying, the job was finished and he stood back to check what he'd done. Written in reverse on the glass, in black outline with pillar-box red infill, were four back to front letters, two on each window, that read:

ЯO OИ

Seb put the red can down, thinking that, if Martin didn't get the message now, he'd have to resort to physical violence. Or something. He peeled off the rubber gloves, dropping them on the ground, imagining Martin's reaction when he eventually got to the flat in the morning. He was about to run back to the alley and exit the scene of the crime when he saw, out of the corner of his eye, a flashing blue light over the other side of the wall. Plod. Had someone seen him and called the cops, or was this just some horrible coincidence and there was a real job going on somewhere else nearby? Whichever it was, he had to find another way out and he had to find it quick.

He couldn't go either of the obvious routes at the side of the flats because that's where the cops would likely be coming from, if they were coming at all. That they might not be wasn't a risk he was prepared to take. Looking around he took in for the first time that the rear of the building faced a small communal garden with fairly dense bushes running all the way down one side to the back wall. If he hid in there and worked his way down, he could probably make it over the wall into the next garden and he'd be away.

He was about to run across the paved area between him and the bushes when he saw a man, crouched down just like he was, staring at him from some three metres away. For a split second he thought he was seeing things, like some weird waking nightmare, as the other person was also dressed in a very similar way to him. Then the man spoke and the spell was broken.

'You're not the law, right?'

'No.' Seb shook his head.

'What the fuck're you doing here then?'

'Getting the fuck out.'

'I'd like to know how, there are two cars, one at the side, one at the front.'

'I'm going the back way.'

Picking up the cans with the discarded rubber gloves, Seb lobbed the lot over to the opposite side of the garden, then dashed across the paving and pushed his way into the bushes. Like he'd hoped, behind the thick outer leaf cover there was a small but fairly clear crawl space going all the way down to the back wall. A couple of seconds after he'd disappeared into the hedge the other man joined him.

'Clever,' he grinned, giving Seb the thumbs-up as he shoved his way in. Moments later they saw the ice-bright beam of a torch cut through the dense leaves. The man put his finger to his lips and Seb held his breath.

The two constables had spent a couple of minutes poking around and it wasn't at all clear from their conversation whether it was Seb or the burglar who was the reason the police had been called. One of the officers found the gloves and cans the other side of the garden and had arrived at the conclusion their quarry had heard them coming and somehow managed to do a bunk. The other one couldn't work out why someone would go to all the trouble of spraying the back window of a flat.

'Koon? What's it mean? ' Seb heard him say.

'Dipshit,' came the reply. 'It's backwards, isn't it; it says "NO OK", right?'

'If you've got something to say, you got phones, you got e-mail and even the bloody post.' The first cop sounded bored, fed up, his voice getting quieter as he walked off, presumably back to the main road. 'What's the point of doing this?'

'That's it, isn't it . . . they're making a point, aren't they.'

In the silence that followed their departure, Seb shrugged at his companion, a thin, wiry man, probably in his late 20s, who smelled quite strongly of old sweat and tobacco. 'Wonder who called them?'

'Shit happens . . . there was zilch in the place I was doing over anyway.'

'What's your name?'

'Don't be stupid, this isn't some bleeding social club!' the man hissed back at him, breath smelling like an old pub ashtray. 'I don't want to know jack about you and what you're up to, and vice versa, mate. OK?'

'Sure, sure.'

'Right, let's make like a Russian and fuckoffski.'

They crawled down through the bushes till they came to the wall, and then it was a simple job to get up and over it, go through the neighbouring house's garden and be out, home free. Standing in the shadows, the man scoped out the street before going, and Seb saw over his shoulder that the light in the flat above the shops had gone out. And then, without a word, the man was gone. Waiting for a couple of beats, Seb exited the driveway, going the other way; hugging the wall until he was opposite another road, he dashed between two parked cars and moments later was far enough from events to feel relatively safe.

As he made his way home, Seb wondered what would happen next. He hadn't considered that the police might get involved, but now they were. It didn't appear that they'd thought it worth waking the occupants of the flat – who weren't there anyway – to tell them about the spraying, probably figuring it could wait till morning. Martin would surely guess who'd done it, but Seb was pretty sure he wouldn't grass him up – the last thing the twat'd want is him being interviewed by the cops. He reckoned he could probably expect at least another phone call and more than likely, at some point, a visit from Dumber and Dumbest.

Although he hadn't solved anything, he did feel better for taking some action, rather than just waiting to see what Martin would do next. He couldn't believe that, on top of everything else, he had to deal with crap like this, but he really did only have himself to blame. Seb had to admit he was a bit of an expert at taking one step in the wrong direction and ending up in deepest shit.

CHAPTER 20

THE ALARM CLOCK WENT BALLISTIC AT TEN TO nine because he'd gone and forgotten to turn it off. And, as he hadn't actually got to bed till about a quarter to five, Seb felt like shit, bleary-eyed and not at all ready to rise or shine. No change there, then. Ella, on the other hand, was as bright as you like. She was also starving and completely not prepared to go down to the kitchen on her own to get some breakfast. Seb had no choice but to get up now, and hopefully grab some extra zeds later.

'Where'd you go last night?' Ella asked him when he came back from the bathroom, where he'd buried his head in a sink full of cold water and felt that bit more awake. She saw him frown and went on, 'I woke up to go to the loo and you weren't there . . . it was about half three.'

'At half three I was either just finishing spraying something on the window of a ground-floor flat, or I was shitting myself cos I thought I was about to be collared by the law. One or the other.'

'Oh. You didn't get caught, then?'

Seb raised his arms in a here-I-am gesture. 'Call me Houdini.'

'Call you a bloody idiot . . . was it that bloke Martin?' Seb nodded. 'You trying to piss him off?'

'I've already done that by telling him I didn't want to work for him; I just thought he might get the message louder and clearer if I sprayed it on his window. I did it back to front so he could read it properly from the inside.'

'Nice touch.'

'I thought so.'

'By the way, Seb . . . '

'Yeah?'

'Thanks again for, you know . . . for last night.'

Seb reached out, took Ella's hands and pulled her up from the edge of the bed, where she'd been sitting. 'Breakfast,' he said. 'Nothing more, nothing less.'

After cereal, toast and tea they went back up to his room with a packet of biscuits and a carton of juice, put a CD on and sat for a while just listening. Then Seb checked his e-mail. Ninety-seven pieces of junk mail; so nice to be popular. After that he remembered his phone probably needed charging and, once he'd plugged it in, he checked the call log because he hadn't turned it on since he was on the bus yesterday. A dozen missed calls, all from the same number. Martin. That guy just never gave up. Seb could imagine him slumped in his flash leather chair, riding the remote with one hand and hitting the redial button on his mobile with the other. Sad git.

'What're you gonna do about him?' Ella had found Seb's GameBoy and was playing one of his old Zelda cartridges.

'Martin?'

'No, the Dalai Lama.'

'OK, OK . . . I dunno, forget about him for the moment and get on with the rest of my life. Got enough to do without worrying about him.'

'Lucky you.'

'What d'you mean?'

'I wish I knew what the hell *I* was going to do with the rest of my life – you know, like after my parents come back from Thailand?'

'You being sarky?'

'No, just realistic; I've got to sort something out, haven't I? Get a job, find a room somewhere, try to clear some shit out of my head and *get* a life to get on with.'

'What kind of job d'you want?'

'I haven't got much choice, with my qualifications it's gonna be some shit minimum wage McJob.'

'What've you got?'

'How d'you mean?'

'Qualifications, how many?'

'Nine GCSEs . . . bunked off after that, didn't do anything else.'

'More than some I know – we could do you a CV,' Seb nodded at his computer, 'look in the local papers, see what's going and send it out.'

'Great CV I'm going to have, aren't I . . . what're you gonna put under work experience – hooker?'

Seb hadn't been ignoring how Ella had spent the last couple of months, but this was the first time the two of them had been faced with the reality in a way that couldn't be brushed aside and dealt with later. He looked at her, sitting on his bed, shoes kicked off and propped up against the wall, leaning against the pillows.

Ella was wearing the jeans they'd bought yesterday and had borrowed a T-shirt and bowling shirt of his; her hair was down, the hunted, pinched expression gone from her face. She was relaxed.

'You weren't a hooker. They *made* you do that, right? You left the moment you could, didn't you.'

'Are you making excuses for me?' She didn't look quite so relaxed now, sitting forward and putting the GameBoy down. 'Cos I don't need anyone to do that, Seb.'

'I'm not making excuses for anyone . . . look, that was then, Ella, this is now, right?'

'You make it sound so easy, don't you.' Ella leant over and took a biscuit. 'But that's because you've always *had* it easy, always had someone there to talk to; even if you'd been the hardest bastard you'd still have had them there, whether you wanted them or not. I bet, no matter how much of a little sod you've been, your parents have tried to understand, right? Try living with someone who doesn't give a fuck.'

Seb didn't say anything. Not that he couldn't think of anything to say, just that he suspected he'd come off sounding like a moron if he did. A moron with his head up his arse.

'I need some space.' Ella broke the stand-off by sitting up and unhooking her bag from the back of the door. 'I'm going for a walk.'

'By yourself?'

'Yeah.'

'Right . . . I'll give you keys.'

'You won't be here?'

'I'll be here.'

'I won't be long . . . look, we've been in each other's faces for almost a solid 24 hours, Seb. I need time to think, OK?'

'Take my mobile, you know, just in case.'

Ella looked about to say no, but changed her mind. 'All right.'

*　　*　　*

After he'd shut the door behind her, Seb stood in the hall in the silent, empty house. Why was everything so bloody complicated? All he'd suggested was that they do a CV so she could apply for a sodding job, and what did he get back? A poor-little-rich-boy character assessment. Well, fuck it. He wasn't poor, little, rich or a boy.

Back in his room he sat in front of his computer and wondered what the hell to do next. He still couldn't believe he'd been so near to making contact with Jay Brill and then had the opportunity snatched from him, like a gust of wind taking away a scrap of paper. He reran the incident in his head, looking at the drawing on the pinboard as he did so; was it the same person, or was he just fooling himself with a false hope? He had to admit that the man on the platform hadn't looked like your bog standard street person, but then Billy, when he wasn't pissed, didn't either. And why had he been standing there with that flower? The way his luck was going, thought Seb, he'd never know anything about Jay Brill, including why he'd saved him.

His eyes drifted away from Billy's drawing and he found himself staring at the rubbish on the floor, amongst which was a flyer pack he'd been given when he'd been coming out of a club earlier on in the year. Inside the clear plastic bag he could see the wad of ads, flyers and stickers it was stuffed with; he picked it up and flicked through the contents, picking out a couple of the stickers. He'd seen them all over the place in the West End – they were basically just an image with a web address.

Seb turned back to his computer and logged back on to the Net. If other people could sticker places and hope they'd get loads of people to contact them, why shouldn't he put up stickers and get one person to contact him? Once his server had fired up he logged on to Hotmail. Even though he already had a Hotmail address, he felt like he should have one just for Jay Brill to contact.

But what should he call it? What would attract Mr Brill's attention? How the hell did he know, he'd never met the guy, had he? Didn't know anything about him. Although he had a suspicion, a mad little idea that just wouldn't go away. He entered all his details and then typed in 'angel' when asked what name he'd like. Back came the answer that it was already taken. Big surprise, but you never knew till you tried. So he kept on trying until he got lucky with angelz129. So that was the address,angelz129@hotmail.com. All he had to do now was design a sticker.

Two hours later Seb had finally got a design he thought would catch the eye, and that was readable from some way off. The floor of his room was covered in all the versions it had taken to get there, and he was standing in the middle of the mess, looking at the latest print-out he'd pinned up, when the phone started ringing in the kitchen.

He ran down the stairs three at a time, cursing his dad for refusing to get a cordless, or at the very least an extension upstairs. He said he wasn't being mean or anything, although Seb reckoned that must have at least something to do with it because the phone they did have was so old it still said 01 on the dial; his dad maintained it was that he had enough of phones at work, and the more phones you had the more tied to them you were. Seb wasn't convinced.

Swinging round the newel post at the bottom of the stairs, he skidded into the kitchen and grabbed the phone just as the answering machine kicked in. Over the top of the message he could hear Martin's voice.

'Don't hang up, I know you're there, sunshine.'

Seb just stood, holding the phone to his ear, his brain in hyperdrive. Martin was having him *watched*? How mad was this going to get? The answerphone message ended and all he could now hear was breathing. 'What d'you want?' he said.

'You know what I want.'

'I don't want to deal for you any more, Martin, got other stuff I have to do. I told Adam and Steve the other day . . . thanks, but no thanks.'

'And left a little message for me last night, too. Not appreciated. Kelly was not amused in a big way.'

'Don't know what you're talking about.'

'You want to wise up.'

'About what? Why are you hassling me, Martin? There must be loads of people out there who'd queue up to work for you.'

'We got a deal, Seb, simple as that . . . you can't walk out on a deal.'

'No *way* do we have a deal!'

'Wanna bet? You come up and have a talk tomorrow morning and certain security film won't get handed over to Lily Law.'

'Sorry?' Seb suddenly broke out in a sweat – security cameras?

'You don't do what I want and you bloody will be.'

'Fuck off . . . '

'And take good care of that nice new girly of yours.'

The phone went dead and Seb was left looking at the receiver – Martin knew about Ella! He looked at his watch and suddenly realised how long she'd been gone . . . he wouldn't have done anything to her, would he? Some part of his brain registered a loud click as the answering machine turned itself off, but it would be some time later before the full significance of what had just happened dawned on him.

Like the phone, the answering machine was another antiquated piece of technology that hadn't been replaced because, as his dad was so fond of saying, if it ain't broke, don't fix it. It was the size of a large book and used two standard cassettes, one for an outgoing message and the other to tape calls, but, once it had picked up it kept taping for three minutes unless you physically turned it off. And he hadn't turned it off.

CHAPTER 21

U P UNTIL THE PHONE CALL, SEB HADN'T REALLY thought of Martin as being anything other than a slightly crazed nuisance who would eventually get bored and go away. He wondered which of his own products he'd been abusing to fry his circuitry so badly, or whether he'd always been an obsessive. Thinking about it now – and realising it was probably not exactly the right time to be doing it – he should've figured that someone like Martin would have had some kind of surveillance. It'd never even occurred to him to look.

So, he had him on film. Or claimed he had. Did he feel like calling his bluff? Right now Seb wasn't at all sure he was, but actually, right now he was more worried about Ella. If Martin was having the house watched it was more than likely he was using Adam and Steve – so it was also likely that he hadn't been imagining things and had spotted them as he and Ella were coming home yesterday.

But what should he do?

'I'm such a . . . !' He slapped his forehead and grabbed the phone. 'She's got my bloody mobile . . . '

The one thing his dad had done that was at least a bit sensible with the phone was to replace the original arm's-length cord with one of those jumbo monsters you see on old American sitcoms. After punching in his mobile number he walked over to the kitchen table where he'd left his cigarettes and was about to light up; he wasn't supposed to, but under the circs . . . and then Ella picked up.

'Where are you?'

'Jesus, Seb, did we get *married* or something?'

'Sorry, I mean . . . look, I just got off the phone from Martin and he knows about you.'

'So?'

'He's making threats . . . there was a CCTV camera outside his flat and he says if I don't do what he wants he'll hand the tape over to the cops.'

'And what did he say about me?'

'He said I should take good care of you . . . I just got worried when I realised how long you'd been out, cos he's had that pond scum Adam and Steve watching this place and . . . '

'Calm down, Seb, I'll come back now and we'll figure something out . . . it'll be OK.'

'How far away are you?'

'Not far, just the library. It seemed like as good a place as any to sit and think about stuff.'

'See you in a minute then, and keep an eye out for a couple of dopers who think they're hard.'

'The harder they come, Seb.' Ella cut the connection and Seb put his unlit cigarette back in the pack.

What he needed right now was a way out, because the hard reality was that if Martin really had a tape, and he handed it over to the cops, Seb wasn't going to have an easy time explaining himself.

He was about to go back upstairs and finish printing out his stickers when he noticed a small red light winking, over by the phone. The light that meant there was a message on the answer machine. He frowned. Then he walked over and pressed 'play', hardly daring to hope what he might hear coming out of the crappy little mono speaker.

'Don't hang up, I know you're there, sunshine.'

He stood, motionless by the machine, as the whole conversation replayed. Everything. From the implication that Martin wanted to involve Seb in his drug dealing business through to his open threats that if he didn't do what he was told he'd be in trouble. What was this called? He'd read it somewhere . . . yeah, a Mexican standoff – he had the tape, Martin had the video, and neither could use the information they had on the other. Neat. The first thing he had to do was make some copies and get them stashed somewhere safe.

He was upstairs rooting round his bedroom for some spare tapes, and had just found an unopened pack when he heard the front door open.

'That you?'

'That's me.'

Seb came out on to the landing and saw Ella down in the hallway. 'Everything OK?'

'Yeah, and you were right about that Adam and Steve. Thick as shit.'

'You saw them?'

'Saw them? They practically introduced themselves!'

'How d'you mean?'

'They were just *so* bad at following me, I spotted them straightaway.'

'Did they do anything?'

'No.'

'Were you spooked?'

'No . . . what're the tapes for?'

175

'Right, right! You gotta come and listen to this, Ella!' Seb legged it down the stairs, rewound the tape in the answer machine and stared intently at it as the message played back again. When it had finished he looked up at Ella and smiled. 'What d'you think?'

'I think he's fucked.'

'Me too,' Seb nodded, turning the machine off, taking the message tape out and replacing it with a new blank.

'Shouldn't that thing be in a museum?'

'Thank God it wasn't.'

'Didn't he know he was being taped?'

'Look, even *I* didn't know he was being taped, I got to the phone just as the machine kicked in and forgot it was on.'

Ella went over to the worktop and picked up the kettle. 'Can I make us a pot of tea?'

'Top.'

'Where's the teabags?'

'That cupboard, left of the sink.' Seb pointed then went and got a carton of milk out of the fridge and unhooked a couple of mugs from the dresser.

Ella filled the kettle and switched it on. 'Got any idea why he's so fixated on having you on his team?'

'The only thing I can think of is that he's just used to getting his own way all the time.'

'Spoilt brat syndrome?'

'Yeah, cos I don't think it's my devastating good looks and awesome wit, somehow.'

'You never know.' Ella cracked the half-smile he was beginning to recognise as her way of saying she thought he'd said something funny. 'What're you gonna do now?'

'Let him know I've got the tape?'

'Good plan.'

176

'Really?'

'Yeah, really . . . '

In the end Seb made three copies of the tape using the hi-speed dub facility on his dad's stereo set-up – a massive complex of hi-fi separates he'd bought when 'real studio' styling was in vogue. Coming out of the big Celestion speakers up on the wall, Martin sounded like a second-rate Hannibal Lecter, all wheezy and kind of put-on creepy, and Seb was surprised at how calm he sounded himself. Not at all like he'd felt at the time.

Having got the copies, the problem was what to do with them next. Did he phone Martin and tell him he'd got the tape? Probably not, as a surprise would be better. Post it? Might get lost. Hand deliver? Might get seen and confronted. And what about the copies – what to do with them? Once Martin knew about the tape, mightn't he send someone looking for the original and any dupes?

It was fairly obvious that Martin's organisation was made up of more than just Adam and Steve – he was simply using kids to sell to kids – and there was no telling who else might be around. So it wouldn't be cool to keep the copies at home in case someone decided to come and have a look.

'Trouble is, though,' said Ella, 'even if you find somewhere out of the house to hide them, Martin's not gonna know that, is he? Still gonna think they're here.'

'Any ideas?'

A couple of hours later there were two packages on the kitchen table waiting to be posted. In one was a copy of the tape, along with an unsigned laser-printed letter;

anonymous, totally meaningless if you weren't in the loop.

Martin. Take no for an answer. Leave me, my friends and family alone or the original of this tape will be sent to the police. The original tape and all copies have been sent somewhere safe.

'D'you think he'll believe me?' Seb was writing his cousin's address on the bigger of the two packages. Eddy, his dad's brother's oldest kid, who was almost the same age as Seb, had said he'd be only too happy to look after the package, no questions asked.

'Only one way to find out.' Ella got up. 'Let's go and register these suckers – where's the nearest post office?'

'Hang on, I gotta put the sticker on the other one.' Seb picked up the second package, peeled off an address label and stuck it on the front. The fact that he had no idea of Martin's surname wasn't perfect, but then very little ever was.

There was no sign of anyone watching them on their way to the post office, where it seemed like every single person in the long line of people waiting to be served was ancient, deaf, had a complex postal problem or some combination of the three conditions. Seb felt he'd aged himself by the time he and Ella came out. He was about to suggest they go for a beer when Ella nudged him.

'Don't look now, but Beavis and Butthead are over the road in that scuzzy kebab place.'

A moment later he looked, and there they were, sitting at the little table in the window and pretending to read the menu. 'How crap are they?'

Ella stepped off the pavement. 'Let's have a laugh.'

Before Seb had a chance to ask how, she was already halfway across the road and obviously making straight for the kebab place. He had no choice but to follow, and caught up with her as she was about to go in.

'What're you up to?'

'Just pulling their chains.'

'I thought pissing people off was stupid.'

'A girl can change her mind.' Ella pushed the door open and walked over to the table where Steve and Adam were sitting opposite each other and sat down next to Steve on the bench seat. 'Hi, my name's Ella . . . which one of you's which?'

'Hello Adam.' Seb sat next to him, patting his back as he did so. 'How's it going, Stevie?'

Trapped and having no idea what to do next, neither of them said anything.

'They always this talkative, Seb?'

'Normally full of it.'

'Eh, boys, you want salad an' hot sauce on both?' Everyone looked round to see the man behind the counter grinning at them, holding a doner kebab in each hand. He looked like he hadn't shaved for a few days, and the stubble on his face joined up with the thick black hair rising like low scrub out of his open shirt collar. 'It's not that difficult, boys . . . yes or no?'

'Give 'em everything. And a couple of extra Cokes for us on their bill.' Seb turned to Adam. 'Thanks for the drinks Ad, we'll be seeing you.'

'If we don't see you first,' smiled Ella, getting up, 'which is quite likely.'

Seb went to the counter and picked up the two cans the man had put there before going to load up the doners with shredded cabbage, sliced tomatoes and chilli sauce. The cans were warm, but actually drinking them wasn't really the point of the exercise. 'Say hi to Martin,' he said, holding the door open for Ella.

CHAPTER 22

VEILED THREATS WERE ONE THING, BUT ONCE Martin got his parcel things might take a very different turn. On their way home, Seb ran the idea past Ella that it was probably about time he had a quiet word with his dad about what had happened, leaving out a few little details he really didn't need to know about, like getting wrecked out in the nature reserve. No need to muddy the water any more than it already had been, and hopefully no need to involve his mum.

'What d'you think he's going to say, your dad?'

'Who knows, he could have a shit-fit with me, insist he goes round and has a quiet word with Martin himself, anything . . . I'm just going to have to bite the bullet.'

'Got a temper, has he?'

'Not really, just gets himself properly stressed out sometimes.'

'And you don't think your mum could handle it?'

'What, that some drug baron's like gonna break into her house and ransack it? No, not really.'

'She seems quite cool.'

'My mum's OK, when she isn't completely on my case or treating me like I was a total kid. Drives me nuts sometimes.'

'Right.'

'Right what?'

'Nothing, Seb. What did you say you were going to do with all those stickers you've printed out?'

'Changing the subject?'

Ella gave him the sideways look, tight-lipped.

'OK, OK – I'm going to go back up west and kind of flyer round places where Jay Brill might see them . . . see them and, you know, get in touch.'

'When're you going?'

'Thought I'd go up now.' Ella looked away, so Seb moved round into her line of sight. 'Didn't ask you cos I didn't think you'd want to come.'

'I don't.'

'I won't be long.'

'Just be fucking careful, OK?'

Seb wondered if he'd ever be able to go into the West End again without getting terminal butterflies. Ella hadn't looked particularly happy about him going, but it had to be done. He'd left her sitting on the stairs saying she was going to find a book to read. Not hard in his house, the place was full of them, not that he'd read one himself for ages.

Stickering in broad daylight wasn't the brightest move, but he didn't have much choice if he wanted to get his message out there as fast as possible. Starting in Leicester Square tube, putting some on both Northern Line platforms and a few more on the up and down escalators, he looked across the tunnel as he rode back up the second time, seeing his message stuck on the spaces between the ads:

JAY BRILL – contact angelz129@hotmail.com

Somehow it'd had more meaning back in his room, and he had to admit that, when you saw it out in the real world, it didn't look like much. But it was all he had.

Leaving the station, he then struck out into the fringes of Soho and round the edges of Covent Garden. No one took much notice of him as he put the coloured labels on phone-box doors, BT junction boxes, lamp posts and parking-ticket dispensers until he'd run out. There was almost nowhere that wasn't already stickered; everywhere you looked seemed to have generations of paper on it, layer after layer of decaying information washed away by the rain, torn off by people who didn't want it to be there in the first place, covered by more recent additions. His own contribution was just more noise and he knew, deep down, that it was very unlikely it would ever get heard.

And all the time he was walking, he kept an eye out for both Jay Brill and Billy Swift. He still felt guilty about walking away from Billy the day before – he really didn't feel he had a scale by which he judged people's worth, but Ella's comment still stung – and he hoped he could find Billy when he was sober, just to maintain contact. But neither of the two people he was searching for were anywhere to be seen. It was one of those things, he figured, like an absolute truth, that, no matter how hard you looked, people only got found when they wanted to be found. But even so, that didn't mean you could stop looking.

It was around seven when he ran out of his labels. Time to go home. But he was hungry now, so before he went back down the tube Seb bought a Crunchie bar and went and sat on some steps for a moment. Someone had left an early edition of the *Evening Standard* there and he picked it up and scanned the headlines as he ate the sweet.

Flicking through the stories, he found nothing he was vaguely interested in, even on the back pages; whichever way you looked at it, most of what was in any paper nowadays couldn't really be called news. He stuffed the paper in his backpack for something to look at on the train and finished his snack watching the crowds surge past him, a solid river of people that he was soon going to have to dive into.

Seb screwed up the empty wrapper, threw it behind him and got up. He wondered how Ella was and thought about calling, but the last thing he wanted was some sarky crack like the last time he'd rung to see if she was OK. Then he remembered about having a word with his dad. Not something he wanted to do, but he couldn't risk leaving it for another day. Martin, he had a pretty good idea, wasn't the kind of person who liked taking his own medicine.

By the time he got home he was knackered. His lack of sleep was catching up with him and he felt like making it a very early night, although having to have the talk with his dad would probably put the lid on that idea. A mug of coffee was called for, no doubt about it. But the sight that greeted him in the kitchen took his mind off the caffeine hit he'd been planning. His mum and Ella, deep in conversation, stopped him dead in his tracks.

'Are you all right, Seb?' His mother frowned at him, concerned.

'I'm fine, Mum, really . . . ' He looked at Ella, who looked straight back at him. No clues.

'Cup of tea?'

'Don't worry Mum, I told you, I'm fine.'

'I'm not worried, I was just asking . . . '

'I fancy a cup of coffee, actually.'

'Fine.'

'Anyone else want one?'

Seb's mum got up from the table, looking slightly pinched. 'I've got to go and check my e-mails,' she muttered, leaving the room.

'Check her e-mails?'

'Just an excuse to leave the room, Seb.' Ella picked up a cigarette end from the ashtray in front of her and carefully moved the ash and other fag ends into a neat pile. 'Why d'you give her such a hard time, she didn't *say* anything.'

'You guys been smoking – both of you?'

'Yeah, and so what?' Ella leant forward on the table. 'I'm not taking sides just by talking.'

Seb hated it when someone could read him like a book, as if he had his thoughts running across his forehead in red dot-matrix letters. 'What did I say?'

'Nothing, and I think I will have a cup of coffee, please.' Ella got up and brought the ashtray over and emptied it in the bin under the sink. 'How did the stickering go?'

'I think I should do some more, finish the job off tomorrow.'

'Did you, like, see anybody?'

'The whole bloody world, and no one I knew.'

After dinner Ella asked Seb's mum if she could help clear up, while Seb asked his dad if he'd come up to his room as he needed to ask his advice about Leonardo man. The plan worked like clockwork.

They discussed various things about the piece for five or six minutes, Seb sitting on the edge of the bed, his dad on the computer chair, and then Seb stood up.

'Dad?' His father turned away from the artwork leaning up

against the wall and looked at him. 'I need to tell you about something, and you're not going to be very pleased.'

Seb's dad sat back in the chair and studied him for a moment. 'Is it something to do with Ella? Is she pregnant?'

'No, Dad, nothing like that.'

'What then?'

How do you tell your dad – who you've only just really started properly talking to, after you've nearly ended up dead through your own stupidity – that you've been stupid for your country again? There was no point in wasting time by trying to paint a prettier picture, best to lay everything out and see what happened.

It didn't take long, because he didn't go into too much detail, and Seb's dad kept quiet until he'd finished. He didn't say anything for a few minutes afterwards, either, and then took a deep breath. Seb held his. Waiting for sentence to be passed.

'I think if I hadn't seen you really start to work during the last few weeks, and watched you produce some impressive stuff, I'd be even more worried about you than I am – and I am worried. This man has CCTV footage of you vandalising his property . . . '

'Which he can't use,' interrupted Seb, ''cos of the tape *I've* got of *him* threatening me and Ella.'

'Very neat, and *very* lucky,' Seb's dad sat forward, 'but what would you be doing right now if the machine hadn't been switched on?'

'Shitting myself?'

'Quite likely.'

'What'm I gonna do if he doesn't believe me that the tapes aren't in the house, Dad?'

'How stupid is this man?'

'I never said he was stupid, I just said he was a bit of a doper obsessive, and like Ella said, a spoilt brat.'

'And you think he's interested in you because you've got more smarts than, um . . . ?' Seb's dad snapped his fingers as he tried to remember something.

'Adam and Steve?' Seb prompted. 'Yeah.'

'So he's not going to believe you're bright enough to get the tapes off the premises?'

Seb sat down. Kind of made sense, what his dad had said. 'So we needn't worry? D'you have to tell Mum?'

'I don't think we have to worry too much about him breaking in, no, but I think you have to worry a hell of a lot about staying well clear of this whole set up.' Seb's dad sat forward in the chair, leaning an elbow on his loosely crossed legs. 'Everything you can say at a time like this sounds so bloody clichéd, but you still have to say it; you only have one turn on the roundabout Seb, OK? So don't, if you'll pardon my French, fuck it up. You've got a good brain, don't misuse it, do something with it other than hanging around with losers. And I won't tell your mum, but from now on, you tell *me* if you think something's going to happen, right?'

'Yeah,' Seb nodded, looking at his feet.

'And think about what you're going to do *before* you bloody well do it . . . you're not stupid, you should've learned that lesson by now . . . and one other thing.'

'What?'

'I don't want to have a conversation like this again.'

'Right.'

'You look like you could do with one of your mum's cigarettes.'

Seb's head snapped back up in total surprise. 'You know about that?'

'I do now.'

'Dad!'

'Only kidding . . . course I know, I haven't completely lost my sense of smell.'

'So why don't you tell her you know?'

'I think it'd spoil her fun.'

Seb looked at his dad, wondering if it was being married to the same person for decades that turned you weird, and then it hit him. 'There is one other thing.'

'And what might that be?'

'He wants me to go up to see him tomorrow morning.'

His dad thought for a moment, then stood up. 'Don't go . . . and if he calls you *after* he's got the parcel, call me at the office and we'll, uh, well I don't know what we'll do, but just call me, OK?'

'Sure.'

That night Seb and Ella slept in the same bed again, alone together. And this time it was Seb who fell asleep almost immediately, leaving Ella strangely aware of Billy Swift's drawing of Jay Brill, watching over them.

CHAPTER 23

WAKING EARLY, EVEN THOUGH IT WASN'T A DAY he had to go to college and he really could do with a lie-in, Seb slid out of bed and went downstairs to the kitchen. He was starving, as he hadn't had much appetite the night before, nervous about the talk he'd been planning to have with his dad. Which, he had to say, hadn't been half as bad as he'd imagined it was going to be. He'd no idea why his dad had been so reasonable, but was very glad it hadn't, as had happened for far less, ended up in a red-faced shouting match.

While he made breakfast for himself and Ella, he kept glancing over at the phone, wondering when the post would arrive at Martin's, worrying what he'd do when he played the tape and realised he'd been outmanoeuvred. Worrying didn't help, just took your mind off what you were supposed to be doing and made you burn the toast. When he'd finally constructed the perfect breakfast, Seb loaded up a tray and took it back upstairs, waking Ella when he closed the door more loudly than he intended.

'Room service?' She yawned, rolling over to look at him. 'How civilised.'

'Didn't mean to wake you.'

'It's OK . . . what's on the agenda today?'

'More stickers, remember?'

'Oh yeah.'

'Don't worry.'

Ella sat up, yawning again. 'Can't help it . . . have you checked your e-mail?'

'E-mail?'

'Angelz129?'

'Jeezus . . . ' Seb gave the tray to Ella. 'I completely forgot!'

Firing up his computer, Seb waited impatiently, a piece of toast and honey in one hand and a cup of tea in the other, while everything loaded and he could log on. That was the trouble with hand-me-down computers, you always got the technology that had been state-of-the-art a couple of years before and now was anything but.

Finally Seb was able to log on to Hotmail, sign in, type his password and access his mailbox. He'd forgotten to turn on the junk filter for the new address and, even though it hadn't even been live for a whole day, there were almost 70 e-mails waiting for him. He knew from experience that they were likely to all be for various get rich quick, get out of debt, get thinner schemes and scams, plus, of course, the inevitable porn sites. In there somewhere might be a message from Jay Brill, so he couldn't simply dump all the rubbish without checking through it carefully first.

Before he did anything he activated the junk filter and put it on 'high'. He couldn't help wondering why, if Hotmail could figure out what was junk mail in the first place, they didn't simply zap it on arrival, rather than sending it on to you and making you do it. Having activated his defences he began trawling through the stuff in his mailbox, while Ella sat cross-legged on the bed and read the *Standard* Seb'd brought back with him the night before.

By the time he'd finished he'd had to delete everything. He had received nothing from Jay Brill, but Ella had found a small ad in the paper from a temp agency saying they were looking for more secretarial staff to go on their books.

'I've got a bit of shorthand, I can kind of type and I can keep a reasonably straight face,' Ella said, putting the paper down.

'Why would you have to do that?'

'Cos I'm not very good at either and I'm gonna have to lie – anything in your mailbox?'

'Nothing I wanted,' Seb reached over and took the last piece of toast, 'so I'd better get printing those stickers.'

'Can I use the phone to ring these people?'

'Go for it.'

Ella stopped at the door. 'D'you reckon he's got the post yet?'

'No news is good news . . .'

Ten minutes later, while Seb was still trying to find a pair of clean matching socks, Ella came back, looking mildly dazed.

'What's up?'

'They want to see me this afternoon. 3.30.'

'Where are they?'

'Southgate?'

'A bus ride.' He looked at Ella, chewing her thumb nail. 'This is good, right?'

'Yeah . . .'

'Look happy then.'

'I've got to take a fucking test! Typing and stuff . . . I'm so going to screw this up.'

'So let's practise.' Seb nodded at the computer. 'There's a computer, we got pens and paper – I'll dictate, you type and scribble. We've got four hours before we have to leave to catch the bus.'

'There you go again, making everything sound like it was as easy as falling off a log.'

'It's a talent . . . now get typing.' He got up and waved her to sit down in front of the computer.

'But what about your stickering?'

'Mañana, it'll wait . . . it's not as if there aren't any out there already.'

At quarter to three they left the house to go and get the bus. Ella nervous, quiet, hiding behind her sunglasses; Seb just happy to be out of the house and away from the phone. Martin still hadn't called, and he was beginning to allow himself to think that he was home free when he saw the familiar figures of Adam and Steve walking towards them from down the road. His stomach sank. He didn't need this and he really didn't need it now.

'The bad pennies,' muttered Ella. 'Ignore them and they might go away.'

'Now you're making things sound easy.' Seb could feel himself tensing as they approached Adam and Steve, his body getting ready while his mind tried to decide whether it would be fight or flight.

'Just coming to see you.' Adam stopped a few metres from them down the pavement. 'Message from Martin, Sebbo.'

'He couldn't phone?'

Adam ignored the comment, but Seb could see that Steve was trying not to grin. 'He said to say that he's fucked off, but it's a deal.'

'Really fucked off – he broke that cassette with his bare . . . '

'Will you *shut it* Stevie?' Adam's eyes flicked between Seb and Ella. 'OK?'

'That it?' Seb could feel his heart pounding.

'Yeah.'

'OK then . . . see you around, guys.'

Seb could feel them looking at him all the way down the road, but he wouldn't allow himself to turn round. That would be like letting the losers score points. No way.

They got back around five o'clock. It had been a good afternoon; even though Ella hadn't done so brilliantly at her tests, she'd done well enough to be signed up on the proviso that she come back in a week and show a reasonable improvement. Not great, not a job, yet, but a whole lot better than being shown the door.

It had now been a couple of days since Seb had done anything to Leonardo man and straight after supper he mumbled his thanks and disappeared upstairs, determined to put in some solid hours threading silk. He was standing on a chair, looping a long piece of emerald-green yarn around a series of black nails up at the top of the piece, when Ella came in and sat down on the bed, observing him at work.

Seb had put a CD on his mini-system and Ella got up to look at the cover. It was sitting on a clear plastic folder full of print-outs, which she picked up instead of the crystal case.

'What's this?'

Seb looked round. 'Stuff I downloaded from the Net. Stuff on angels.'

'Mind if I have a look?'

'Go ahead . . . in fact I haven't even read it myself yet.

193

You could tell me what I've got, I just printed out anything that looked interesting.'

Ella sat back down and started leafing through the pages. Almost immediately she stopped at one, pulling it out to read.

'Did you know that the word angel comes from the Greek word *angelos*?'

'Sounds logical.'

'And that angelos means messenger.'

'Really?' Seb looked round at her.

'Really. D'you think Mr Brill had a message for you?'

'Mobile phones can seriously damage your health?'

'Be serious.'

Ella went back to her reading and Seb carried on weaving different coloured threads in intricate patterns across the mass of nails, pulling them taut and tying them off in a tight knot. Then he stopped; frowning, he looked over at Ella.

'Did I tell you, you know, that Jay Brill has Greek letters tattooed on his arms?'

'No.'

'Well, he does.' Seb pointed over at the drawing on the pinboard. 'He's got an alpha on his right arm and this one called zeta on the other . . . they're an a and a zed.'

'Yeah?'

'D'you think it means something?'

'Honestly, Seb,' Ella riffled through the paper on her lap, 'could mean anything, everything, nothing . . . I dunno.'

'Only way I'm ever gonna find out is by asking him, isn't it?'

'I'd say . . . '

Seb went back to his threading, every so often moving as

far back as he could get in the room to find a new perspective on what he'd done, occasionally asking Ella what she thought. She, for her part, read him out the bits of information she thought he'd find interesting, like the fact that it wasn't just Christians who believed in angels, they appeared in Jewish, Muslim and Indian religions as well.

'And it says here on this bizarro God-is-a-spaceman site that the angel Gabriel is often portrayed holding a lily.'

Seb stopped what he was doing. 'Say that again.'

'The angel Gabriel is often shown with a lily in his hands.'

'Lilies are white, aren't they?' Ella nodded. 'Like the one . . . '

'Like the one that man on the tube platform was holding.'

'That man who looked like Billy's drawing of Jay?'

'Must be a coincidence, Seb, right?'

'Why?'

'I dunno . . . cos otherwise it's all just too freaky.'

Right then there was a knock on the door; Seb walked over and opened it to find his dad outside.

'Got a moment?'

'Many.' Seb moved back to let his dad in. 'What's up?'

'Didn't get a chance before supper to ask, Seb . . . any news on the Martin front?'

He glanced over at Ella. 'We bumped into those two guys, Adam and Steve? They said that Martin was pissed off, but that it was a deal.'

Ella shifted forward on the bed. 'They said he was so pissed off he broke the cassette with his bare hands.'

'Sorted then.' Seb's dad looked over at Leonardo man. 'That's really coming along now; nearly finished?'

'Day or so, I reckon.'

'All we've got to do then is get it up to school.'

Seb looked at the massive piece. 'Hope it's not raining, otherwise we're gonna need a bloody great plastic bag.'

Smiling at the thought, Seb's dad waved as he softly closed the door behind him.

Ella sat back and picked up a couple of sheets of paper that had been stapled together and started to read. 'He's taken all the Martin stuff very calmly.'

'Don't tell me.' Seb picked up a new piece of thread. 'I can't quite get my head round it, like why he hasn't gone mental?' There was no reply from Ella, and Seb glanced over to see what she was doing. He thought she looked a bit pale, but supposed that could just be the light. 'You all right?'

Ella looked up at him, frowning slightly, chewing her lower lip. 'Get your head round this.'

'What?' Seb sat down on the edge of the bed.

'You visited an Islamic site, right?'

'If you say so, I don't remember . . . I was going through Google, opening up stuff and printing out anything that looked interesting.'

'You never read any of it?'

'No, I told you. Why?'

'W-e-e-ll, it says here, right, that the Arabic form of Gabriel is, um . . . '

'Is what?'

'Is Jabril.' Ella turned the page to show him where it was printed.

'Jay Brill?' whispered Seb, shaking his head. 'But that's not possible. Is it?'

'Jesus, Seb . . . I dunno.' Ella reached over and squeezed his hand. 'Wanna go outside – cigarette break?'

'Yeah, OK . . . fuck, this is weird, Ella, this is *so* weird.'

'There's got to be an explanation, right?'

'What if there isn't? What if . . . ' Seb stopped. He wasn't sure he actually wanted to say what he was thinking out loud. Out loud made it all somehow more real.

'What if?'

'Like . . . what if he, you know, Jay Brill, really *is* an angel? What then?'

'God knows . . . no, I mean I didn't mean it like that, not a joke – I don't *know* what it means, Seb. It doesn't *have* to mean anything, except to you. No reason for anyone else to know.'

'You do.'

'Trust me, I'm not going to go round shouting about that I might've seen an angel.'

'Makes me wonder even more why he chose to help me . . . ' Seb stood up and stared at the drawing on his pinboard, walking over till he was standing only inches from it. 'If I wake up and all this has been just a dream, and I don't find out what the *hell* is going on, I am *so* going to be fucked off.'

CHAPTER 24

X-RATED!!! GIRLS, GIRLS, GIRLS!!! NUDE LIKE never before!!! Books, mags, vids!!! All the fluorescent signs in the windows were on, flashing their messages to a world that, right now, mostly had other things on its mind. Come dusk, people would be in the mood to look and be lured, but at this hour the effect was severely muted by the fact that it was broad daylight. Seb was back up west.

He'd wanted to drop everything the previous night and go right there and then, but Ella had pleaded with him to wait till the morning. He'd hardly slept, he was so strung out about the information he'd downloaded so many days ago and that Ella had just found. It had been there all the time, if only he'd taken a moment to look! He felt like kicking himself, although what difference it would have made, knowing what he knew now any earlier, he hadn't quite worked out.

This time Seb not only had more stickers, he'd brought a stat of Billy's drawing and another of the sketches of the tattooed symbols with him. He was on a mission. Somewhere out there was a man who might be called Jay Brill, who might be an angel, who the only thing he knew about for sure was that he'd saved his life. And he had to find him. He had to.

When he wasn't stickering, he was showing the drawings to everyone he could find: shopkeepers, buskers, office workers, anyone who might recognise either the face or the tattoos or both. Nothing. He was talking to the caff owner where he'd stopped for a cup of tea and a fried egg sandwich, about to get out the stats, when he saw a policeman walk by outside the shop and he was pulled right back to when he was in another caff with Billy Swift. Billy had asked him why he hadn't gone to the cops to find out more about the man he was looking for, and he'd said something about that being the last resort. Which was now. Now was about as last resort as it got.

The last time he'd tried to go and talk to the police was the day he'd found himself standing across the street, staring at a girl he thought was called Crazy Janey and who turned out to be called Ella. He wondered what would happen this time.

His walk over to the Charing Cross police station in Agar Street turned out to be completely uneventful. The place wasn't some faceless red brick and glass building like he'd expected; instead, its calm, pale exterior looked more like a library than a cop shop. He walked up the steps into the cool lobby, all glazed tile and dark wood; there were a couple of people in there, sitting on opposite sides of the room on bench seats smoothed by decades of waiting. Seb went over to the reception and stood while the officer there finished his phone call.

In the heavy silence of the lobby the click of the handset being replaced in its cradle was very loud. 'Can I help you?'

'I was, um, beaten up a couple of months ago, over by Embankment tube? This station dealt with it.'

'Sorry to hear that – you all right now?' Seb nodded. 'What can I do to help?'

'Someone, a man, saved my life that night, but I can't find him to say thank you – I know his name and what he looks like,' Seb pulled Billy's drawing out of his backpack, 'but I don't know where he lives or anything.'

'And?'

'Well, I thought there might be a record, some note taken at the time that would give me his address.'

'More than likely there was, but I certainly can't give that out, and,' he looked at his watch, 'the officer who was in charge is down at Bow Street, won't be back today. You'll have to come back tomorrow, have a chat with him then; best I can do, OK?'

Seb looked away, unable to hide his disappointment.

'Take this number.' He looked back to see the officer holding out a card. 'Ring before you come down, make sure he's here.'

'Thanks.'

He was standing outside the police station, wondering what the hell to do next, when his mobile rang. Home. He cancelled the call. Didn't feel like talking right then, to anyone, his mum, his dad or Ella. With no idea where to go, he just wandered aimlessly, down the Strand, around Trafalgar Square and past the National Gallery. On the way his phone rang from home twice more and twice more he cut it off, finally relenting on the fourth call.

'Yeah?'

'Seb! Why weren't you answering?' It was Ella, sounding frantic, and he suddenly felt guilty about not picking up.

'It's OK, Ella – everything's OK.'

'Where are you?'

'Near Leicester Square.'

'What happened?'

'Nothing happened, nothing at all . . . no one's seen him or recognises him and the only policeman who might be able to help won't be around till tomorrow. I just got a bit pissed off, didn't want to talk to anybody, that's all.'

'Come back, then?'

'Yeah.' Seb looked at his watch: 5.15; he should be home within the hour. 'I'll see you soon.'

Instead of turning and walking back past the National Gallery and taking the direct route to the tube, Seb decided to weave through the back streets instead. Kind of on auto-pilot, letting his internal compass guide him, he wasn't really paying attention to exactly where he was or what was going on around him. In his head he was thinking about Ella.

Were his parents aware that they probably weren't acting like your normal lovey-dovey new boyfriend/girlfriend? Which they weren't, because they weren't lovey-dovey new boyfriend/girlfriend. Although they had, over the last few days, become much closer. And where would that lead to? How long could you spend in the same bed as someone else – someone like Ella – without something occurring? Or maybe not. He had to admit that she fascinated him, he was attracted to her personality, her combination of strength of character and fragile emotions. He liked her. She liked him. Did it mean any more than that?

Confusion. Turmoil. Uncertainty. All too bloody complicated.

He was dragged back to street level by the all-too familiar sound of a fight kicking off, and he looked around to see what was happening. Up ahead, on the other side of the street, he could see two blokes having a real go at a third man, really kicking the holy shit out of him, all the time shouting something about him being filth. Fascination moved him forward, while self-preservation kept him from crossing the road. Recognition stopped him dead, like his batteries had been taken out.

One of the men dealing out the blows was Zack. How could he forget the cruel, slitted eyes, the sallow, waxy skin and wide, thin-lipped mouth?

Rooted to the spot, Seb, who'd run through the 'meeting-Zack-in-the-street' scenario so many times he almost felt like it had already happened, was paralysed. He knew he should go and help, at least try and even up the odds, except the voice in his head kept on saying 'but it's *Zack*, man – he's a fucking maniac!'

And then he saw Zack's accomplice truly belt the guy, watched him fall to the ground behind a parked car and saw Zack bend down. Saw Zack stand up, dragging the man off the pavement. Watched as he waited for a second, then flung the man out into the path of an oncoming car. Couldn't believe his eyes as he saw the limp body bounce off the bonnet, the car screeching to a halt.

Seb was aware that Zack and his friend were legging it away, that the driver was getting out of his car and, like a magnet, the incident was drawing a crowd of curious onlookers. His mobile was already in his hand as he made the decision not to chase after Zack and he was dialling 999 as he ran towards the body on the ground. What could this guy possibly have done to make Zack want to try and kill him?

'Which service do you require?'

'Ambulance . . . please.'

'Could you give me details of the incident?'

'Road accident, someone pushed in front of a car.'

'Where?'

'It's in . . . ' Seb looked around for a street sign, momentarily glancing down at the man on the ground, his body twisted in an awkward, unnatural shape.

'Are you still there, sir?'

Seb found himself looking at Billy Swift.

'If you're not going to answer, you'll have to get off the line.'

Billy Swift?

Seb cancelled the call and stuffed the phone in his pocket. Kneeling down, he could see Billy's face was covered in blood, but he couldn't tell whether it was from his beating or hitting the car.

'I didn't have a chance to stop – he just came running out into the road!' The driver of the car, not seeming to be talking to anyone in particular, was standing nearby but not too close, like he was in danger of catching something.

Seb looked up at him. 'Call an ambulance.'

'I thought you'd just done that, weren't you just on the phone?'

'Call a fucking ambulance!'

'OK, OK . . . ' The man turned his back on Seb.

It was obvious that Billy was in a really bad way. Seb could now see that most of the blood was coming from a serious head wound, and Billy was hardly conscious, eyelids fluttering, breathing shallow. He knew he shouldn't move him, but he couldn't stand around and do nothing.

'It's OK, Billy,' he reached out and held Billy's cold hand, 'you'll be fine . . . ambulance'll be here soon, mate.'

As he strained to hear evidence that he wasn't lying, that there actually were sirens in the distance, he let go of Billy's hand and shrugged off his cotton jacket. The least he could do was try and keep him warm. Before he laid the coat over him, Seb gingerly picked Billy's left hand up to lay it on his chest and as he did so the sleeve of Billy's shirt rode up his forearm, uncovering part of a faded blue mark.

A tattoo.

Seb pushed the sleeve further up to reveal a looping zeta symbol, just like the one he had on the stat in his pocket. He shivered, feeling like tiny, ice-cold spiders were marching up his neck, and his scalp tightened on to his skull, shrinking as if in fear of being pulled off. Slowly, he leant over and pulled up the sleeve on Billy's right arm, knowing what he was going to see, but not understanding entirely what it meant. Confused, because he didn't know whether he wanted to be right.

But the alpha symbol was there, a misty imprint, washed-out and pale, but visible nonetheless. And there was only one thing it could mean. Billy Swift was Jay Brill. Jay was Billy.

Nothing made sense.

How could it? He'd seen Jay Brill on the tube, hadn't he – the man in Billy's drawing? And then there was the flower, the name, all the stuff on the Net that made it true. But then if Billy was Jay, and if he was an angel, why would an angel lie? Even if he *wasn't* an angel, why would he lie? So many bloody questions, no reasonable answers. Nothing made sense, any kind of sense at all.

Seb covered Billy with his coat. 'Billy?' He saw Billy's eyes flicker at the sound of his whispered name. 'Who are you Billy? I've got to know . . . '

He felt a light tap on his shoulder and turned to see the driver, pallid and nervous. 'They said they'd be here any minute . . . police are coming too, someone said they saw him being pushed into the road.'

'He was.'

'You saw it too? Thank God.'

Seb turned back to Billy; frightened he might say something that he'd miss, he bent down again. 'You're not on your own, Billy, I'm here . . . it's me, Seb.' He glanced round to see if anyone was listening. 'Billy?' Urgent, whispered. 'You got to tell me . . . why me, Billy? Why d'you choose *me*, why d'you choose to save me? You knew everything, so why me?'

Billy stirred, and Seb leaned in even closer. Nothing.

'Please Billy, I've gotta know why – why didn't you tell me? And Billy . . . are you an angel, Billy?' Seb saw his lips moving; at first he couldn't hear anything, then softly, like something half-remembered in his head, he heard words.

'They call us lonely . . . ' Billy paused and Seb thought that was it, ' . . . when we're really just alone . . . '

CHAPTER 25

YELLOW-JACKETED PARAMEDICS PUSHED THEIR WAY through the crowd, two of them, a man and a woman. Seb hadn't even heard the ambulance arrive. He was still so completely dazed by the sudden revelation of Billy's identity and the fact that, even though he'd found him, there were still no answers; part of his head was finding it easier to believe he was asleep and dreaming, that any minute he'd wake up.

The woman knelt down by Billy, gently moving Seb out of the way so she could get in and take a closer look. He stood, looking down on the scene, like he was the cameraman in the middle of some fly-on-the-wall docudrama. He found himself focusing on the woman's dyed-blonde hair, noticing that her dark roots were showing; he was very aware of how young the male paramedic looked, not much older than him, and he could see, with icy clarity, his badly-bitten fingernails.

Time didn't stand still, like people said it did, but for Seb it travelled at different speeds. The world outside the circle of bystanders was still as fast-lane as it ever was, but inside the warp of the attention bubble it was definitely slower.

'Is this your coat?'

For a moment Seb didn't realise he was being spoken to.

'Sorry? What?'

'Is this your coat?' The male paramedic was holding up Seb's jacket while the woman was covering Billy with a blanket.

'Yeah . . . thanks.' Seb took it. 'Is he, like gonna be all right?'

'He a friend of yours?'

Seb nodded.

'Honest answer, I don't know, mate . . . '

'Get the board and a neck brace, Bry . . . we've got to get him out of here quick, I can hardly feel his pulse.'

Seb watched the man as he legged it to the back of the ambulance and he saw that the police had arrived as well. A constable was talking to the driver, who right at that moment turned and pointed at him. It wasn't done in an accusing way, but it still made him feel oddly guilty as the policeman glanced his way and then began to walk over to him.

Before he got there, the paramedic arrived back carrying a long, narrow plank and an oddly shaped piece of plastic, which he gave to his colleague. Seb watched as she roughly measured Billy's neck, made some adjustments to what he now realised was the collar she'd asked for, and then carefully fitted it.

'I gather you saw the incident, sir.'

Sir? Seb looked round and found the PC standing next to him. 'Yeah, I did, all of it.'

'Could I take some details?'

Seb watched as the two paramedics gingerly slid the plank under Billy and then saw the man go off again. 'Sorry?'

'Some details, what exactly did you see?'

'There was a fight? I heard, like a fight kick off and I saw a guy called Zack and another bloke beating on Billy . . . '

'You know their names?'

'Yeah, one of them's called Zack, and this guy, he's called . . . ' Seb pointed at Billy and stopped. What was he called? He saw the man who he'd always known as Billy Swift, still couldn't believe might be Jay Brill, being carefully lifted up on to the trolley, which the man had wheeled back and then collapsed to almost ground level. 'I'm pretty sure his name's, um, Billy . . . Billy Swift. Look, he's a kind of friend of mine, I've gotta go with him to the hospital.'

'Hold it.' The constable put out a hand to stop Seb. 'I need your details too.'

'Seb Mitchell . . . ' The paramedics were strapping Billy to the trolley as he gave the PC his address and phone number.

'OK, we'll be in touch.'

Seb went over to the paramedics as they lifted the trolley up to waist height, made sure it was locked and were about to go. 'Can I come with him, he's a friend.'

'Angie?' The man looked from Seb to the blonde woman and she nodded. Seb followed them round to the back of the ambulance.

The doors had slammed shut, the siren and flashing lights turned on and the ambulance began moving slowly at first, gathering speed as its urgent howl alerted traffic to get out the way.

The woman, Angie, leant forward. 'You'd better jump some lights and get us blued in, Bry . . . ' She glanced over at Seb. 'Your friend's going to need all the help he can get.'

*   *   *

His friend.

Seb was suddenly aware of the synchronicity of the situation he now found himself in. Him and Billy in an ambulance. Again. Only the last time it was him covered in blood and all strapped down. Only the last time Billy had saved his life.

All he'd done was watch.

He could still hear the voice in his head . . . *'It's Zack, man – he's a fucking maniac!'* . . . and couldn't get the image out of his head of Billy being stomped on, lifted and thrown into the path of a car. He felt sick with guilt, like he could throw up from swallowing so much shame, the acid bile rising in his throat.

'You OK?'

Seb focused on Angie. 'Not really.'

'I know it sounds stupid, but try not to worry. It doesn't help.'

'Sure.'

'What's his name?' Angie picked up a clipboard and pulled the biro out from under the clip.

'Billy, Billy Swift.' Seb took a deep breath. 'Where are we going?'

'UCH, off Tottenham Court Road.' She peered out of a window. 'Not too far to go now.'

'Hold on, Angie,' Bry called out from the front, 'fast right coming up!'

Angie put the clipboard down as the ambulance slewed round the corner, tyres squealing, rolling like a boat on its suspension, and Seb grabbed the edge of his seat and braced his feet, leaning against the force trying to throw him sideways.

'You'll stick around when we get there, yeah?' Angie

peered at Billy, reaching over for his wrist.

'Sure,' Seb nodded. 'Where do I wait, in Casualty?'

'Yeah . . . just let the nurses at the station know who you're waiting for . . . shit!'

Seb saw Angie lean forward, her ear close to Billy's blood covered face. 'What's the matter?'

'Bry, I think I've lost him!'

'We're there, Angie, we're there!'

Moments later the ambulance came to a halt and Seb heard Bry leap out and run round to the back as Angie began pumping Billy's chest with the crossed palms of her hands.

'Hurry up, Bry . . . ' The doors opened. 'No pulse, nothing . . . '

'Let's get him in PDQ.' Bry began pulling the trolley forward, its legs dropping and locking, Angie following, still trying to get Billy breathing again, and they were gone. Sitting in the back of the ambulance Seb could hear Bry yelling something, like he was shouting for a doctor, and then the silence whistled in his ears; he could hear the last words Billy had spoken, about thinking you were lonely, when you were really just alone. Right then he felt both.

'Hey you!' Seb glanced round to see a nurse standing, hands on hips, looking at him. 'Seb, isn't it? What're *you* doing here?'

It took a second or two for Seb to remember who she was, then a name came back to fit the face. 'Nurse Owen?'

'Well your memory seems to be fine, and you look 100% better than the last time I saw you . . . there's nothing wrong, is there?'

'Not with me.'

'Who then?'

'It, um, it's too weird, really.'

'Try me.'

'That man, the one who came in here with me? You know when I got . . . when I nearly died?' Seb was finding it hard to talk, his throat closing up as if he were being strangled by the grief he was feeling at having watched Billy die. His fault, in a way, because he'd done nothing to stop Zack from throwing Billy in front of the car. Nothing at all.

'What Seb?'

'I think I found him. He's here, they took him into Casualty, but I think he's dead . . . I'm waiting to find out.'

'You're *sure* it's the same person?'

'Even if it isn't, I still kind of know him . . . I told you it was weird.'

'How long have you been here?'

Seb looked at his watch. It was 7.35, over two hours since he'd told Ella he'd be home soon. Fuck.

'Seb?'

'I've been waiting about an hour and a half – where do I have to go to use my phone around here?'

'Just go out front . . . would you like me to try and find out about your friend?'

'Could you?'

'Course, what's his name?'

'Billy Swift, that's what he should be booked in under, anyway.'

'Look, we've just been told there's been a bad fire up in Camden somewhere and we're expecting ambulances any time . . . it's going to be busy in here. I'll get back to you as soon as I can, OK?'

'Sure.'

Seb went out of the building and turned his phone back

on; it showed he had missed some calls and immediately began to ring. The answering service. Two messages, both, unsurprisingly, from Ella. He dialled and the phone was picked up almost before it rang.

'Hello?'

'It's me, Ella.'

'Seb?'

'Yeah, sorry I didn't call before . . . I couldn't.'

'Where are you, what's the matter?' Silence. 'You still there?'

Where to bloody start. Seb had no idea what to say. 'Look, it's complicated, big time, OK? I've got to hang round for a bit more, but I'm fine, really . . . I'll explain everything when I see you. And don't worry, it won't help.'

He cut the call before Ella could say anything else and then turned off the phone. He really didn't feel he could talk about what had happened, or where he was, on a mobile. It was going to be hard enough doing it face to face. And he knew he was blanking most of the last hour and a half, knew he'd have to deal with the reality eventually, but right now somehow preferred the limbo of not *actually* knowing what he couldn't quite believe to be true.

As he turned to walk back into the Casualty waiting room Seb heard the strident wail of an ambulance — no, two ambulances — and saw them come in. He felt like one of those disaster voyeurs watching, so he went back inside to see if Nurse Owen was back with any news. There was no sign of her anywhere so he went over to the station to see if either of the people there, the ones who booked people in if they were just ordinary, nothing special emergencies, had seen her. They hadn't.

'Can you page her, or anything?'

'She'll be out soon, no doubt.' The woman, whose name badge said she was called Marie, didn't look at him as she spoke.

'Can you tell me anything about what's happening to my friend?'

Marie looked over her glasses at Seb. 'What was his name?'

'Billy Swift.'

The woman shook her head, tapped a couple of keys and peered at the screen in front of her. 'Can't see him here, not under William either . . . maybe he's not been booked in yet – he came in code blue, didn't he?'

Seb nodded. 'They called in from the ambulance.'

'Probably it then . . . ' Marie raised her eyebrows.

'What?' Seb frowned at her.

'He was that RTA, wasn't he, bad head injuries?'

'RTA?'

'Road traffic accident, sorry.'

'Yeah, only it wasn't an accident.'

'Oh, right . . . '

'He, like died, just as we got here? I just wanted to know, you know, for sure . . . '

'I understand, and Nurse Owen was trying to find out for you?' Seb nodded. 'I'll put out a page, but she is on duty, might not be able to get back to you straightaway.'

Seb looked at his watch. 'I'll wait for a bit.'

Seb looked at his watch again. 9.05. He was sitting at the back of the pub, waiting for Ella. He'd texted his mum from outside the tube, asking her to get Ella to meet him; he couldn't face going home, he knew he must look as ragged as he felt and there was no way he could face any parental questioning, no matter how well intentioned.

Nurse Owen hadn't turned up, hadn't sent a message, nothing. But then she was probably up to her neck in burn victims and, although he found it difficult, Seb could see that getting a message to him came some way down the list of 'must do' things under those circumstances. In the end there'd been no point in staying; like the lady at the desk, Marie, had said, phone tomorrow. But then she dealt with tragedy, pain and probably death on a daily basis; he didn't. Walking away from the hospital, not knowing for sure if Billy were dead, or if by some miracle he'd survived, was the hardest thing he'd ever done.

Having failed to help him, he was now abandoning him again, and he felt like a complete shit. A complete shit with no answers and one big fucking question. If Billy was an angel, how could he die?

CHAPTER 26

'ZACK DID IT? YOU SURE IT WAS HIM?' ELLA LOOKED like she'd been punched, left hand clutching her waist, the other one covering her mouth. Seb picked up a cigarette packet from the table between them and offered her one, taking another himself and lighting them both. In the chaos and confusion of the last few hours he'd forgotten quite how close to home this whole thing was for Ella as well.

'Yeah, I'm sure it was him, you don't forget a face like that in a hurry.'

'And Billy *died*?'

'That's what that paramedic said . . . he died in the ambulance, right next to me.'

'Oh Seb . . . ' He looked up to see tears streaming down her face.

'Don't, Ella.' Seb put his fag out and went to sit next to her, putting an arm round her shoulder. She fell against him, like she'd fainted, and sobbed; a couple of people were looking their way, but he didn't care. 'It's OK, Ella, it's OK.'

'It isn't,' she sat up slowly and looked at him, wiping the tears away with the heel of her palm, 'it stinks . . . that *bastard*!'

'I was thinking, on the way home, how weird it was that

everything leads back to that shit Zack?'

'How d'you mean?' Ella got a tissue out of her bag and blew her nose loudly.

'He invents Crazy Janey; I kind of meet you through him. He beats me up and takes all my money, so I go to the soup van looking for a way home, nearly get killed and get saved by Jay or Billy or whatever the hell his name is.' Seb lit another cigarette. 'And there he is again when I finally find Jay or Billy or . . . '

' . . . or whatever the hell his name is.' Ella took Seb's cigarette from between his fingers, took a puff and gave it back. 'As a conspiracy theory it's lacking a bit in, you know, plot?'

'Whatever . . . ' Seb stopped, hit once more by the reality that Billy was dead and he'd never know why anything had happened.

'Seb?'

'What? Oh . . . I dunno, I can't get my head round anything. I mean, if Billy *is* the person who saved me, and those blokes at the soup van saw the tats – they did the bloody drawings of them and they were *exactly* what Billy had – why didn't he say so? Why did he invent Jay Brill and then draw me an incredibly accurate picture of a total stranger? Why?'

'What makes you think he was a stranger?'

Seb's glass stopped half an inch off the table as he let the comment settle on him like a veil, yet another layer of obscurity. 'S'cuse me?'

'Maybe Billy knew him.'

'Nothing made much sense *before* you said that . . . '

'Did it ever?'

'Looking for a man called Jay Brill made *some* kind of

sense,' Seb took a drink, 'but without him there's no reason, there's no point any more.'

'To anything?'

'Well, if it's all just coincidence and chaos, no, not a lot.' Seb looked off at some faraway point, his face suddenly very sad. 'Not if it's all, like, totally fucking *random*.'

'I thought you might understand, Seb.'

'Understand what?'

'You're an artist, isn't that what art's supposed to be all about? Chaos and coincidence? I've spent hours looking at that Leonardo man in your room . . . I love that it looks so totally random, but that there's a pattern underneath, some kind of logic that makes sense depending on where you're looking at it from.'

'You do?'

'Yeah. Like the closer you get, the more intense the randomness?'

'And the further away, the clearer the image . . . ' Seb smiled, nodding.

'Right. And I've been thinking, about Billy.'

'What about Billy?'

'What could he really tell you that would make any difference?'

'The reason why he did it all? That would be good, for starters.'

'And if there wasn't a reason? What then?'

Seb sat back, rubbing his eyes with both hands. 'I've had it.' He got up. 'I'm tired, I'm hungry and my brain hurts.'

What was it his dad said? Everything looks better in the morning? Something along those lines. Crap. Seb felt spaced and wired and like some crucial bits of his head weren't working. He'd slept badly, partly because his head was full of the images, sounds, smells and emotions of what had happened to Billy – of what he hadn't done for Billy. And partly because, he had to admit it, it was getting difficult with Ella, being next to her, close but still in limbo. With the basic instinct monkey tapping on his shoulder, grinning and winking. He'd have to deal with that. Soon.

Seb was standing in the kitchen, looking at the phone in his hand, the dial tone purring away like a demented kitten. Ella was sitting at the table, eating a slice of toast. 'What did the hospital say?'

Seb put the phone down. 'They said,' he shook his head in quiet disbelief, 'they said they had no record of a Billy Swift.'

Ella put down her cup of coffee. 'How come?'

'Remember yesterday, in the ambulance? The woman, what's-her-name, Angie, she asked me Billy's name to fill in some form . . . and then she didn't do it.'

'Why not?'

'The ambulance took a serious right hander and we both had to hang on so's we didn't get chucked about. And then she saw Billy was in trouble and I reckon it never got filled in; Billy probably didn't have any ID on him, how were they gonna know who he was if he couldn't tell them?'

'That can't be it, though.'

'What're they gonna do?'

'But the police, surely they'll be involved? I mean, it's like murder now, right? Zack killed him.'

'They've got my details, I gave a cop my name and everything.'

'Shouldn't you ring them, tell them you know who did it?'

'I already told them,' Seb shook his head. 'He could be

alive, though, Ella . . . I should go down the hospital, find out for sure. It's driving me mad, not knowing for absolute sure. He could be OK, he could be alive, they bring people back all the time, right? I have *got* to bloody know.'

Out of sheer frustration Seb thumped the wall with his fist. And the phone started to ring.

Ella grinned. 'Good trick.'

Seb picked it up. 'Yeah?'

'Need a word, Seb . . . gotta moment?'

'Martin . . . ' Seb's shoulders slumped, he leant back against the wall and shook his head as he looked over at Ella; eyebrows raised, with a 'want a cigarette?' look on her face, she mimed lighting up, and Seb nodded.

'Seb?'

'I'm here.' Seb took the cigarette Ella held out to him. 'What d'you want?'

'I got your package . . . kind of a stalemate, right?'

'Kind of.' Seb could hear the TV shuffling through channels in the background.

'And Kelly's been talking to me.'

Seb waited for a couple of beats. 'Still not happy about the windows?'

'Not delirious, but she saw your point.'

'She did?'

'That's why I'm calling.'

'What did she say?' Seb saw Ella frowning at him and he shrugged 'I've got no idea' back at her.

'Told me to stop obsessing and that there's no point having someone around who doesn't want to be there. So . . . you want out?'

'I want out, like I told you, and Adam and Steve.'

'OK, OK, I heard you.'

'Finally.'

'Right, you all right with that?'

'I'm fine.'

'You don't sound fine, Seb.'

'I'm tired Martin, and I've got to go to the hospital and find out if a friend of mine's dead or not. Kind of puts the lid on your day, you know?'

'Sorry to hear that.'

'Thanks, Martin. Bye . . . ' Seb put the phone down, took a deep breath and let it out slowly.

Ella got up from the table. 'What did he say?'

Seb went past her into the kitchen to empty the ashtray he'd been using. 'Basically, he said there was no point in having someone around who didn't want to be around.'

'So he's gonna stop hassling you?'

'I s'pose I'll have to wait and see about that, but I think I'm out of there.'

As if on cue, the phone started to ring.

Ella looked over her shoulder. 'Want me to get that?'

Seb nodded and Ella picked the phone up.

'Hello? Oh, hello . . . yeah, kind of . . . thanks . . . ' Ella looked over at Seb, smiling her odd little half-smile and nodding as she listened. 'Right, right, I'll tell him . . . OK, goodbye.'

'Who was it?'

'Martin.'

'Martin? What did he want – what was he saying?'

'God, he's weird.' Ella looked at the phone like it was weird as well. 'Does he have the TV on and like change the channels *all* the time?'

'All the time . . . what did he say, Ella?'

Ella looked at her feet. 'He asked me if I was, you

220

know, your girlfriend.'

'He did?'

'Yeah . . . ' Ella looked up, 'and he said that he'd been thinking about it and to tell you that only the good die young . . . that's how it works, he said.'

They sat at the kitchen table, drinking the coffee Ella had made, not speaking for some time. Seb was trying to get his head round the fact that he was finally off the hook with Martin. Kind of just like that. Why? Why, after all the hassle, had he backed off – could it all really be down to Kelly having a go at him? With Martin, anything was possible.

'Know what gets me?' Seb began building a pyramid out of sugarlumps.

'What?'

'There's never any answers, only more questions.'

'That's how it works.'

'Very clever.'

'You going to the hospital, then?' Ella added a sugarlump to Seb's construction.

'Better had, better get going.' Seb sighed and got up. 'D'you know where I left my phone?'

'In your room, by the keyboard.'

'Are you gonna come with me?'

'Want me to?'

'Wouldn't mind.'

'OK.'

'Thanks.'

Seb found himself grinning as he went up the stairs, two at a time, to his bedroom; maybe the trip on the tube would be a good time to talk to Ella about things, because it was neutral territory. He could find out what she'd said when Martin had asked her if she was his new girlfriend. He had a feeling she'd said yes. He picked up his phone, then stopped and looked at the computer screen. Instead of going back downstairs, he sat down and powered up the machine.

'I thought we were going.'

Seb looked round to see Ella standing behind him. 'Realised I hadn't checked the e-mail today . . . won't take long.'

'But why now, what's the point?'

'I dunno.' Seb watched the loading screen clear, then clicked on the Hotmail icon and waited. 'Like I said, it won't take long.'

'Don't be, you know, too disappointed.' Ella picked up her bag and went out.

Seb saw the entry page had loaded and typed in his sign-in name and password. He clicked on the 'Sign in' box and waited again while the steam-powered modem accessed his mailbox. And then there it was. He had 64 messages in his inbox and 187 in his junk mail folder. Seb dumped the junk without even bothering to look at it, then started going through the mail, clicking the 'Block' box as he went down. He was almost at the bottom when he saw it. His mouth went dry, and he swallowed. In the 'From' column was the name Jay Brill, highlighted in blue and underlined.

Seb's hand shook as he held the mouse, unable to open the file, staring at the date. Today. This morning. Finally he managed to move the cursor over the name and clicked the mouse. Up on the screen came the message, a single word. It said, 'Believe'.